CHRISTMAS AT THE VINTAGE BOOKSHOP OF MEMORIES

Elizabeth Holland

Copyright © 2020 Elizabeth Holland

All rights reserved

The characters and events portrayed in this book are fictitious. Any similarity to real persons, living or dead, is coincidental and not intended by the author.

No part of this book may be reproduced, or stored in a retrieval system, or transmitted in any form or by any means, electronic, mechanical, photocopying, recording, or otherwise, without express written permission of the publisher.

Cover design by: Dawn Cox Photography

ABOUT ELIZABETH HOLLAND

Elizabeth Holland is a keen writer of romance novels. She enjoys the escapism of picking up a book and transporting yourself into a new world. With her mind bursting with lots of different stories, Elizabeth is exploring the world of self-publishing her novels. She started writing when her mental health was at an all-time low and it helped her to cope.

The Balance Between Life and Death is Elizabeth's first novella. Elizabeth suffers with anxiety. She wanted her first novella to focus on mental health (with a side helping of romance). This story is a reminder that you never know what someone else is going through. Elizabeth's second book was The Vintage Bookshop of Memories - a feel-good romance.

CHAPTER ONE

The antique bell rang out as the door to *The Vintage Bookshop of Memories* opened. Nobody looked up as a fiery redhead stumbled through the doorway, with a light dusting of snow covering her entire being. She placed her suitcase in the nook behind the door. Her presence had gone unnoticed. Everyone's attention had been stolen by the assortment of books that surrounded them. Nobody noticed the way she shrunk into her own shadow, avoiding eye contact with any of the customers.

"It's awful out there!" She exclaimed, to no one in particular, as she shook the snow off onto the welcome mat. The inside of the shop was warm and toasty, with the hushed tones of overexcited book shoppers. The red-head unwound the scarf from her neck and placed it on the hook by the door - it would take a while to dry. She then removed her cream coloured coat and hung that up beside the scarf. Underneath her wet outerwear, she was wearing a knitted jumper dress in a rich emerald colour, black tights and brown Chelsea boots. To anyone in the village she would have looked awfully stylish with her bright red hair cascading down her back in perfect ringlets, despite the snow trying to dampen its fiery spirit. However, anyone that knew her would know that her fashionable appearance was more luck than style.

The atmosphere within the bookshop was magical; every

inch exuded Christmas spirit. Sat on the central round table was a small, real Christmas tree, and the pine scent wafting from it was permeating the air. Red and golden ornaments adorned the tree, which glimmered in the light from the chandelier above. Underneath the tree sat an assortment of Christmas themed goodies from gingerbread men to miniature chocolate yule logs. In front of the treats sat a sign informing customers that they were free to enjoy. With a smile on her face, the red-head picked up a gingerbread man and began nibbling at it as her eyes were drawn to the new bunting hanging from the balcony. Hand-stitched Christmas scenes adorned each little triangle. It was beautiful. Even the ladder to the upper floor had ivy wound around it. Towards the back of the shop the children's section housed an array of vintage teddy bears, each wearing a hand-knitted Christmas jumper. The atmosphere within the shop was contagious.

"Katie!" The redhead turned in the direction of the voice to see her best friend, Prue Clemonte, running out of the kitchenette. As Prue made her way over to her, dodging a few customers, Katie took in her appearance. She looked beautiful, as usual, wearing a 1940s red tea dress, pulled in at the waist with a black belt. Her dark hair was cut into a sleek bob, and she'd taken the time to match her lipstick to her dress. Prue had always been the glamorous and stylish one in their friendship. Before she knew it, Prue had thrown her arms around her best friend.

"Prue, I've missed you so much." Katie wrapped her arms around her friend and allowed herself to sink into the embrace. It had been over a year since they had last seen each other. Life had got in the way for both of them.

"How are you?" Prue stepped back and looked at her friend.

She only had to glance at her to know that the smile on her face was false.

"It's been a tough few months." Katie admitted, nervously chewing at the side of her cheek. She really had to stop doing that; the wound would open up again. Being back in Prue's company made Katie wonder why she hadn't confided in her sooner. She had suffered alone.

"Come through to the kitchenette, we'll try to squeeze in there and have a chat. I've got to stick around to sign for a delivery, otherwise I'd take you straight home." Katie couldn't help the smile that crossed her face. Being back in Prue's company instantly made her feel happy. The two women made their way to the little door at the back of the shop.

"Hello, Maggie." Katie waved at the woman sat behind the till. Maggie returned her wave and promised that they would have a cup of tea and a slice of cake later. Katie could already feel her spirits lifting from being back in Ivy Hatch. She was already feeling like the old Katie again. There was something so special about this little village.

Once they had squeezed into the kitchenette, Prue shut the door to give them some privacy.

"Sit down and I'll make you a cup of tea." Prue pointed Katie towards a box in the corner which Katie suspected was full with books. Most likely ones that Prue had forgotten she had ordered and now had no more room on the shelves.

"Thank you." Katie watched in silence as Prue effortlessly navigated the tiny space and made them both a drink before she squeezed onto the box next to Katie.

"Tell me." Prue's smile was reassuring. Katie took a deep breath, ready to tell Prue all about the disastrous few months that she had been having.

"I've been an idiot, Prue," Katie swiped angrily at the rogue tear that was making its way down her face. "After seeing you in Brighton last year, I threw myself into work at a new gallery and quickly became best friends with my boss. I thought she was brilliant and we had a real laugh together. I looked forward to going to work every day. That is, until I found her in bed with my boyfriend."

Prue gasped in shock as she put her tea down and wrapped her arms around her friend.

"Why didn't you tell me?" She asked, giving Katie a final squeeze before letting go.

"You've been so happy lately, with the auction house and with Elliot, I didn't want to involve you in my disastrous world. To be honest, I think it might have been for the best. The longer I'm away from Zac, the happier I feel." Katie took a deep breath to stop the tears from coming. She didn't want to spend her first day with Prue crying on her shoulder. Prue had been through enough over the last couple of years; losing her grandmother, inheriting the village of Ivy Hatch and proving to everyone that she was reliable. The people of Ivy Hatch had been reluctant to accept Prue as their new landlady, she had been met with hostility, however she had refused to step down. Prue's strength and resolve worked, and eventually the villagers worked with her to create a peaceful and fruitful future for Ivy Hatch.

"Katie, you know I'm always here for you. Whatever is

going on in my life, I'll always be here for you to talk to or even just to cry down the phone to."

"Thank you, Prue. Anyway, I'm single, jobless and homeless. Merry Christmas." Katie let out a dark chuckle that Prue couldn't help but join in with.

"Here's to the future." Prue clinked her mug with Katie's. Prue knew all about leaving the past behind you and she would do everything she could to help Katie look towards the future. One week in Ivy Hatch was all she needed, Prue would soon have her life sorted.

"Anyway, enough about me. I'm here for your wedding and from this point forward that is all we're going to talk about. Pinky promise." Katie kept her face straight as she held out her pinky finger for Prue to shake. It wasn't long before both women dissolved into a fit of giggles.

CHAPTER TWO

Eventually, the book delivery arrived. It was boxes and boxes of second-hand books. Katie shook her head. Her friend hadn't changed, she still loved anything with a past.

"What on earth are you going to do with these?" Katie could hardly believe her eyes as she took in just how many books there were. The shelves within the bookshop were already heaving under the weight of thousands of stories.

"For now, let's just leave the boxes inside and go home. I'll deal with it tomorrow." Prue's smile was infectious. The two women glanced back at the boxes one last time and then made their way to the Clemonte Manor.

To Katie's surprise, Prue led her towards a modern, black, four-wheel drive.

"What happened to the classic cars?" Katie asked, trying to shield herself from the smattering of snow that was falling. Her friend was obsessed with everything vintage, even cars.

"I needed something that was a little more weatherproof." Prue replied, looking at the modern car with disdain in her eyes.

"I'm guessing Elliot insisted on you having a safer set of wheels." Katie laughed as Prue nodded her head. Internally,

Katie sighed, if only she had somebody who cared about her and her safety. Katie knew that deep down Prue appreciated Elliot; she knew how lucky she was to have him by her side. However, Prue was often too busy to show just how much she appreciated him.

They lifted Katie's suitcase into the boot and began their journey up to the manor. Katie couldn't help but marvel at how idyllic the village of Ivy Hatch looked with a light dusting of snow covering it. Christmas songs played quietly from the radio and for the first time in a while Katie felt herself relax. Ivy Hatch was a lifetime apart from Brighton, yet something about it sung to her soul. It was a little bubble of happiness, and Katie needed that. Her eyes wandered to where she knew the craft shop lay. She would visit soon and buy everything she needed to start painting again, it had been a while since she last picked up a paintbrush and she missed it.

"Are you sure you're okay, Katie?" Prue asked, glancing over at the wistful expression on her face.

"I'm fine, I promise. I know I might not look it but I'm happy. I've had a tough time in Brighton and it's nice to be here." Katie threw a reassuring smile towards Prue.

They remained in silence as they drove the rest of the way to the manor, both lost inside their own thoughts.

"Hello?" Prue called, holding open the manor's door for Katie to wheel her suitcase in. There was the sound of raised voices coming from the kitchen, and it seemed that Elliot had not heard Prue's greeting. Together they made their way to the kitchen, the conversation becoming clearer the closer they got.

"I don't want to leave the farm, Elliot!" An unknown voice echoed throughout the house, the tone was filled with anger.

"Why not? Are you going to spend your life working as his servant?" The second voice was Elliot's; he sounded just as angry as the other man.

"We're home!" Prue shouted, this time loud enough for the two men to hear.

"In the kitchen!" Elliot called back, just as they pushed open the door.

"I hope we're not interrupting." Prue smiled warmly at the two men and went to give Elliot a quick kiss. Meanwhile, Katie took in the scene in front of her. The two men had been stood at opposite sides of the breakfast bar. Their faces gave away their inner anger. The man stood opposite Elliot looked almost identical to him and yet somehow he was better looking, at least Katie thought so. His eyes were like storms, dark and tempestuous. Katie was drawn to him, however at this moment in time she didn't quite know why. Yes, he was good-looking, but she had been around many good-looking men in Brighton and not felt this way. Perhaps it was because he looked broken, like her. Two souls in need of saving.

"Of course not. Hello Katie, lovely to see you again." Elliot stepped forward to greet Katie and gave her a quick hug.

"Hi, Elliot!" Katie couldn't help but feel the stresses of the recent weeks lift from her shoulders. She was surrounded by people who loved her and all she wanted was to enjoy the next few weeks.

"Katie, this is my brother, Austin." Katie could barely string together a hello as Elliot introduced her to his brother. She moved forward and accepted Austin's embrace. In those few short moments where he hugged her, she felt her stomach flutter at the possibilities. As she pulled herself away Katie mentally chastised herself - she did not need another man in her life complicating matters. She hadn't even begun to pick up the mess that the last one had left.

"Shall we have some drinks? Austin, are you staying for dinner?" Prue, being the perfect hostess that she was, immediately began throwing together some drinks. Since Katie's last visit, she had turned a corner of the kitchen into a bar area, complete with a gorgeous Art Deco bar cart. The cart was filled with crystal champagne glasses and various bottles of locally sourced gin. It was a gin-lover's heaven and a teetotaller's hell. Katie knew that from this moment up until Christmas, life would be one big party. Perhaps it was what she needed - some fun.

"I'd love to stay, thank you." Austin smiled timidly at Prue. Katie couldn't help but notice the tone of his voice had almost been like a question. As if he were afraid she would say no to him.

"I'd say no to the drink if I were you, mate, Prue fancies herself as a mixologist.' Elliot rolled his eyes at his brother. The previous tension between them had disappeared.

"I'm making my own invention of a cinnamon Christmas cocktail filled with gin." Prue announced as she brandished a golden cocktail umbrella with a maraschino cherry on the end.

"Can I have a beer?" Austin looked afraid that he might be forced to try Prue's concoction.

Prue laughed and pointed Austin in the direction of the fridge, which was filled with various beers and ales. Katie, meanwhile, took the over-the-top cocktail from her friend and took a sip. It was disgusting, but thankfully there was just-enough gin to mask the taste.

"Shall we go into the living room?" Prue suggested before leading the group to the front of the house. Katie gasped as she took in the sight before her - the living room looked beautiful.

On the other side of the room, in front of the floor to ceiling windows, stood a huge Christmas tree. It was adorned with purple and green baubles to match the room's decor. At the top of the tree, proudly sat an angel that looked as though it had been passed down many generations.

Elliot caught her looking at it, "Prue keeps bringing things home from the auction house," he explained, as they both shared an understanding smile. Prue still enjoyed buying vintage items that were filled with people's memories. Katie turned her attention back to the room in front of her. The fireplace was adorned with stockings, each one looked like they had come from the auction house. Katie's favourite was the one hanging right in the middle. It was a patchwork masterpiece and looked Victorian in design.

"That stocking is yours." Prue caught her eye and winked at her. Katie couldn't help but smile back at her friend. Why hadn't she come back to Ivy Hatch sooner? It was just what she needed.

"What one's mine?" Austin asked, taking a seat on one of the two purple velvet sofas. Katie had to avert her eyes before she got lost in the sight of him sat sipping his beer. Who knew a man sitting on a purple velvet sofa could be so attractive?

"I didn't think you'd be here on Christmas Eve?" It wasn't often that Prue Clemonte was taken by surprise, she usually had multiple scenarios planned out in her head and she was ready to act on any of them at any given moment.

"I don't think I'll be spending Christmas at the farm this year." Austin glanced down at his bottle of beer. He looked awkward. The room remained silent for a moment, and Katie inspected Austin's face. His eyes held a glimmer of rejection in them. Katie knew she had to say something. She wanted to watch Austin's face light up again and feel herself drawn to his expressive dark eyes, rather than trying to avoid looking at the pain within them.

"That'll be fine with Prue, it means she gets to buy another stocking." Everybody chuckled at Katie's remark, and the relaxed atmosphere returned to the room.

Prue and Elliot took a seat on the other sofa, leaving the only remaining free space next to Austin. Trying to hide her smile, Katie sat down next to him, careful not to spill her gin over the beautiful fabric. There was just enough space between them to stop Katie from reaching out and laying a hand on his arm. He had looked so dejected when he realised Prue hadn't bought a stocking for him. Katie had to fight her natural instincts and instead of comforting him she took a sip from her drink, scrunching up her face as the flavour flooded her tastebuds. She was here to heal herself, not to fix anyone else's life.

"How do you like being a farmer?" Katie knew that it was an awful question, but she had to fill the silence before her thoughts took over.

"I love it, especially getting to look after the animals. It's a nice feeling to know that they rely on me, and all my hard work and long-days are all for their benefit." Austin was very forthcoming with his answer, so much so that Katie was taken aback. She was unaccustomed to strangers being so chatty, especially towards her.

"I love animals. I'm so happy to hear that you have their best interests at heart." Katie took a deep breath. She had to do better at engaging him in conversation. Why had she started a conversation about animals? It had been a longtime since she had last been single and talking to men. Perhaps it was okay, after all, he was a farmer. Most people liked talking about animals, right? Katie did.

"I must give you a tour, sometime." Austin winked at her, before taking another swig of his beer. Katie did everything she could not to swoon. Was he really flirting with her?

"I'd like that," she replied, winking back at him. Austin was slowly bringing out a side to Katie that she had forgotten existed. Lately, she had become too comfortable with her lack of confidence and resulting shyness. If only she could piece together an adult conversation, then she might find herself falling for him.

"What are you passionate about, Katie Wooster?" Hearing Austin use her full name only made Katie swoon even further. She really was making a fool of herself this evening.

"Art is where my passion lies," she confessed, feeling herself perk up as she crossed into a topic she knew well.

"Is that what you do for work?" Austin asked, he looked genuinely interested in hearing about her.

"Before I came here I worked at an art gallery." Katie cringed as the humiliation crept up on her. She didn't want to think about Brighton and everything that had happened there.

"Is it not what you want to do?" Austin asked, misreading the expression on her face.

"I'd like to paint." Katie blurted it out before she had even thought about the answer.

"Are you good at it?"

"I think so. What about you, are you good at farming?"

"I like to think so. Unfortunately, I can't ask the animals for feedback."

"So do you see yourself still farming in five years time?" Katie wondered if her question was too forward. What right did she have asking Austin about his future plans?

"Hopefully, if I can modernise the farm." He shrugged his shoulders and looked down at the empty beer bottle clasped in his hands.

"What's stopping you?"

"My father." Katie didn't know what to say in response. She had heard a lot about Arnold Harrington and his archaic approach to life. When Prue returned to Ivy Hatch, Arnold didn't agree with her approach to immersing herself in village life. He thought that she should accept her place in society and uphold it. Prue, had other ideas, which only angered Arnold and it cumulated in him receiving a criminal record and losing both his son and his wife.

"Anyway, tell me more about you. What do you paint?" Austin changed the subject, refocusing the attention back to Katie.

They continued talking about their plans for the future. Their passions shone through as they encouraged one-another. Prue and Elliot watched on in silence.

CHAPTER THREE

As Katie opened her eyes, she squinted against the bright light that was pouring in from the curtains that, in her drunken stupor, she had forgotten to close. It wasn't often that Katie drank. In Brighton she was usually the designated driver. It suited her boring persona - at least that was what Zac had told her. As Katie lay there, waiting for the room to stop spinning, she couldn't help but let her mind reflect on the previous evening. She knew that she ought to be concentrating on herself and getting over the ordeal that she had gone through in Brighton, but she couldn't help but be charmed by Austin. They had spent most of the evening chatting and laughing. She had learned all about his life on the farm. He wanted to modernise the farm and his father was refusing to implement any of the changes. It appeared that Arnold Harrington hadn't changed much since Katie's last visit. He was still the foul-mannered brute that he had been when Prue returned to Ivy Hatch.

As Austin spoke his passion for his work and the animals in his care had immediately captured Katie's heart. As the drinks had kept coming, Katie told him how she was out of work and possibly homeless due to having recently moved in with her cheating ex. Austin had listened to her and comforted her, however Katie soon realised that she was enjoying the comfort not because she was upset but because she enjoyed being lavished with Austin's attention.

Katie threw an arm over her eyes and groaned. She really hoped she hadn't embarrassed herself last night. In hindsight, she had giggled a little too much at Austin's jokes and touched his arm on a number of occasions. With a sigh, Katie resigned herself to getting out of bed. Anything would be better than lying there, wondering what a fool she had made of herself. As she sat up in bed, Katie took a moment to appreciate the guest bedroom that Prue had prepared for her. The four poster bed had ivy wrapped around each post and hanging at the end was some mistletoe. Katie rolled her eyes at the sight. It was highly unlikely she would kiss anybody over the festive period.

"Morning!" Prue called as Katie entered the kitchen. She was far too happy for a Sunday morning which was accompanied by a hangover.

"Morning," Katie winced as she pulled herself up onto one of the breakfast bar stools.

"Bacon sandwich?" Prue questioned, holding the pan out to emphasise her question.

"Yes, please! How are you so chirpy?"

"I was up at the crack of dawn. Elliot gave Austin a lift back to the farm. I think they're going to speak to their father."

"What's going on there?" Katie asked as she grabbed the coffee pot and poured herself a cup. Usually she hated coffee - it was too bitter - however she needed something to get rid of this dreadful hangover.

"Arnold's refusing to move with the times. Elliot and I have talked about possibly giving Austin one of the neighbouring farms. He knows what he's doing, and he has big plans.

It's not fair on him to have Arnold holding him back." Katie couldn't help but notice the protective edge to Prue's voice. She was already a firm part of Elliot's family. Katie felt a pang of envy. She had her own family, but they were far too caught up in their own lives to worry about her. Katie reminded herself that it hadn't always been like that for Prue. She had only recently found her father, Robert, and they were still slowly building a relationship.

Prue placed the sandwich down in front of her and Katie tucked in, feeling the coffee slowly working its caffeinated magic on her head.

"Are you excited for today?" Prue asked. She was almost bouncing up and down on the stool, watching Katie eat. They were going shopping today for Prue's wedding dress and Katie's bridesmaid dress.

"I will be once I've eaten this and had a shower." If Katie was honest, she wasn't particularly excited about their trip to the shops. She didn't share Prue's love for fashion. However, she would do whatever it took to make her friend's wedding day perfect.

After breakfast, Katie had a quick shower and began to feel her senses return as the pounding in her head eased. In future she would pour her own measures of gin, Prue's were lethal. As Katie stood in her room with a towel wrapped around her, she looked longingly down at the dress she had worn yesterday. It was comfortable and easy to wear but she knew that if she even attempted to wear it again today, Prue would have her back upstairs and into something *fashionable* before she could even begin to protest. With an exasperated sigh, Katie undid her suitcase and tried to find something that wasn't too creased. After a few minutes, she had settled on a pair of black jeans and a grey cable knit jumper. It was plain, which suited Katie. With hair resembling a blazing fire, Katie wasn't too adventurous with colour when it came to clothing.

As Katie met Prue in the hallway, she could see the look of disappointment that crossed Prue's face as she took in Katie's appearance.

"What?" Katie playfully rolled her eyes. She didn't mind Prue's obsession with clothes and enjoyed teasing her.

"I had thought yesterday's dress signalled a change in your style. Perhaps you'll dress up more tonight when you hear who's coming to dinner." Prue's tone was teasing. Katie tried to resist asking who was coming for dinner, but eventually her inquisitive nature won.

"Who's coming for dinner?" Katie asked as she climbed into the passenger side of Prue's modern car. It was still snowing, so they decided not to risk taking one of the classic cars.

"Austin." The word echoed throughout the car as Prue began the drive to the next town. Katie didn't say anything in response. She obviously hadn't masked her feelings very well last night.

"It's okay Katie, it's just because I know you so well. Anyone else would have just thought you were being friendly." Katie breathed a sigh of relief at Prue's reassuring words. She hadn't made a fool of herself... yet.

Eventually, they parked outside a little bridal boutique. It looked perfect for Prue. As they stepped through the door, they were immediately greeted by an older lady brandishing a bottle of champagne. Katie's stomach did a flip at the mere sight of alcohol.

"Welcome ladies, can I interest you in a glass of bubbly whilst you take a look round?" The shop owner had a huge smile across her face.

"I think it's a little early in the day for us." Prue made their excuses and asked if they could have some orange juice instead. The lady left them browsing the dresses while she went to prepare their drinks.

Katie looked through the dresses on display, not really knowing one end from the other. They all looked exactly the same to her. However, for Prue's sake, she was pretending she was interested. This was the easy part. Next they'd be shopping for her dress.

"Oh, this is perfect." Prue's voice was breathless as she held up a dress. Katie turned to look and despite her limited knowledge of fashion, she knew that this dress was Prue's dream dress. It was a white silk dress, which resembled a slip, with panels of lace. The delicate straps at the top had what could only be described as a cape made of tulle. It was like a veil that fell to the floor and trailed behind the dress. It was utterly breathtaking, and Katie knew that Prue would look divine in it.

Katie took a seat, and Prue disappeared into the changing room. As she waited for her to reappear, she watched the people outside the shop. The snow was still falling and people were frantically walking around the streets, trying to pick up last minute Christmas presents. With only a week to go, stress levels were rising. Katie's attention was quickly brought back into the comfort of the bridal shop as Prue emerged from the fitting room. Her breath caught in her throat as Katie took in her appearance - she was sure that this dress had been made for Prue. The dress perfectly skimmed her figure as the tulle cape flowed behind her.

"Oh Prue, you look amazing." Katie gasped as she wiped away a stray tear.

"You like it?" Prue asked, excitedly, her sleek black bob swung around her neck as she jumped up and down in excitement. Katie had never seen her friend in such good spirits.

"Like it? Prue, I love it! What about some lace gloves?" Katie couldn't believe what had just come out of her mouth, even Prue seemed taken back.

"That would be perfect. I'll make a fashionista out of you yet, Katie Wooster." Both girls laughed before Prue tried on a pair of lace gloves. They completed the look.

Prue re-emerged in her own clothes. She had dressed very stylish today with a black velvet coat, complete with a faux fur trim, black tights and black heels. Katie had to stifle a laugh, she really did look like the lady of the manor sometimes. Once Prue had paid for the dress and it was safely stowed in the car, they continued their shopping trip.

"I've already picked out a dress for you." Prue informed Katie as she held open the door to a dress shop to allow Katie to walk in ahead of her.

Before Katie could respond the woman sat behind the till had jumped up and came running towards them.

"Miss Clemonte, sorry I wasn't expecting you for another

half an hour." She apologised before a funny look crossed her face. She almost looked as though she was considering curtsying.

"Sorry, our first appointment was a little quicker than expected. We can pop for a coffee and come back?" Prue's smile was so genuine that Katie couldn't help but smile too. She really was very lucky to have a friend like Prue.

"Oh, no! You girls take a seat and I'll go and grab the dress. I'll be back in a few minutes." The woman dashed off behind a curtain at the back of the shop. Meanwhile, Prue and Katie took a seat on a sofa by the changing rooms.

"Do you like Austin?" Prue asked, breaking the silence that had fallen.

"I don't know him," Katie replied. She could feel her cheeks going red and she felt flustered. Why did Prue have to know her so well?

"I know you, Katie. It only takes you two minutes to meet someone and fall in love with them. I also know that you fall hard. Austin's a good guy and I think you two could be very happy together." Prue reached out and took Katie's hand in hers. It was freezing cold, but Katie didn't mind; the gesture meant a lot.

"I'm scared, Prue. Is it too soon? I'm only just getting over the last heartbreak."

"I think the fact that you're already considering Austin means that you've moved on, Katie. Your ex was never right for you, you knew that as well as I did." Prue had a point. Katie had always felt out of place in Zac's world. Perhaps deep down she had always expected him to leave her for someone else, someone more suited to him.

"Besides, I can see you as a farmer's wife." Prue winked at her just as the lady returned with her bridesmaid dress. Katie glared at Prue as she stood up and followed the woman into the changing room.

As the dress bag was unzipped Katie had to force herself to keep her eyes open. What if she hated it? She took a deep breath to steady her nerves. Prue knew what suited her, it would be fine.

"I'll leave you to get changed, just give me a shout if you need any help." The woman gave her a fleeting smile before leaving her alone with the dress. After taking a deep breath, Katie laid her eyes on the dress that was peeking out of the bag. Immediately, she breathed a sigh of relief. It was emerald green; at least it would look pretty with her hair. As Katie pulled the dress from the bag, she was overcome with emotion - it was truly beautiful. The dress itself was velvet and cut elegantly. It was full length, nipped in at the waist and had a sweetheart neckline. The straps were thin, but it had a similar tulle cape to Prue's dress, only hers doubled as sleeves and ended at the waist. For a girl who didn't like wearing dresses Katie couldn't wait to put it on.

The dress fitted perfectly with the fabric pooling slightly at her feet, giving the effect of her gliding as she walked. Before Katie walked back into the shop, she did a little twirl in front of the mirror. She couldn't help but notice that the sparkle in her eyes had returned - she was feeling excited about the future for the first time in a very long while.

"Is everything okay?" Prue called. She sounded worried.

Katie realised she must have been in there for a while now, just looking at herself in the mirror. It was so unlike her that she had to stifle a giggle.

"It's perfect." Katie announced as she emerged from the changing room. As soon as Prue's eyes fell on her, she saw them fill with unshed tears.

"Oh Katie, you look beautiful." She stood up and embraced her friend.

Fifteen minutes later, Katie's dress was safely stowed in the car next to Prue's.

"Thank you for this, Katie. I know shopping isn't your favourite thing to do, nor is fashion."

"If every dress looked like my bridesmaid one, then I could very quickly find myself enjoying fashion."

"Come on, let me buy you a gingerbread hot chocolate to say thank you for being a good sport." Katie didn't have to be asked twice, she linked her arm through Prue's and together they walked across to the coffee shop.

CHAPTER FOUR

The cafe was charming inside, filled with the history of the little town. The walls were adorned with historical pictures of how the village had changed over the years and nestled in the corner was a box filled with toys that the village's children had outgrown. It was a treasure trove of memories. They chose the table by the window so that they could watch people walk past. A waitress came over to take their order; she must have only been a teenager and looked nervous. Katie smiled at her. She remembered her first job as a waitress; she had been terrified of all the customers. One man had even shouted at her when she brought him over the wrong drink. From that point on, she had always made the effort to be extra nice to anyone serving as she knew what it felt like to be in their shoes.

"Could we have a gingerbread hot chocolate and a gingerbread latte?" The girl smiled back at Katie and the relief was evident on her face - a nice, simple order.

As the waitress left, Katie turned her attention back to Prue. She was staring aimlessly out of the window, her attention looked miles away.

"Last minute wedding jitters?" Katie teased, she knew that there was no way Prue had any reservations over marrying Elliot.

"Oh no, sorry, Katie, I've just been thinking about a conversation I had with Elliot last night." The worry that Prue was feeling was evident on her face.

"What's wrong?" Katie was worried about her friend. After everything she had gone through, when she returned to Ivy Hatch, she wanted her to be happy.

"We're worried about Austin. His father, Arnold, is being such a brute. He refuses to let Austin take any responsibility at the farm and treats him almost like a slave. It's awful, Katie." From the moment Katie met Austin she had liked him, and Prue's revelation had only strengthened her feelings towards him.

Katie was just about to reply when the timid waitress interrupted her. "Your drinks," she said, placing the cups down in front of them. She had got them the wrong way round and so as soon as her back was turned Katie and Prue swapped.

"What can you do to help him?" Katie asked, trying to return to their previous conversation.

"I own a farm on the other side of the village. It's been empty for years so it would need a lot of work. If we offer it to Austin, then Elliot has suggested he take a year's work sabbatical to help Austin."

"That sounds like a brilliant idea!"

"The problem is it would only anger Arnold even more. Since returning to the village I've turned his life upside down and I don't think he'd appreciate me giving Austin his own farm."

The women sat in silence for a few minutes as they considered the situation. Katie took a sip of her hot chocolate and felt her tastebuds explode as memories of Christmas filled her mind. Christmas was a time for giving and she was firmly of the opinion that Prue should allow Austin to rent one of the empty farms.

"Prue, Arnold is never going to change. It's too late for him. Elliot has moved on, he has you and an amazing job. Maggie has your father, and she's loving working at the bookshop. Why should Austin suffer?" Katie was surprised at how passionate she came across. She meant every word. Why should Austin suffer because his father was such a ruffian? After leaving Arnold, Maggie had grown close to Robert and they were tentatively exploring their future together. Meanwhile, Elliot was happy with Prue and focusing on his career as a solicitor. It was time for Austin to leave Arnold's clutches and find his own happiness.

"Oh Katie, I can always count on you for some words of wisdom. What will I do when you leave?" Prue reached out across the table to take Katie's hand in hers.

"Oh, you'll be fine. It's what I'm going to do that's the problem." Katie sighed and stared down at her half-finished hot chocolate, not wanting to meet Prue's eye. Prue would immediately be able to see the distress behind Katie's expression.

"Are you still upset over that idiot of an ex?"

"A little, but it's more than that, Prue. I have no job and nowhere to live." Katie felt the tears collect in her eyes, blurring her vision. She didn't want to cry, today was supposed to be a happy day.

"Katie, you're staying with me until you sort yourself out." It wasn't an offer, it was a statement. Katie smiled weakly at Prue, it was good to know that she had such a strong friend to support her through this.

"Thank you, Prue. I won't stay with you for long. Once Christmas is over, I'll start applying for some jobs and then I can find somewhere new to live."

"There's no rush. In the meantime, why don't you start painting again? You could always try to sell a few. Or if you're really desperate, I can find something for you at the auction house."

"Thank you, Prue. I might try to paint again. Life has been so busy in Brighton that I haven't picked up a brush in years."

Katie felt a little happier having spoken to Prue. She had a plan, she would paint again. Katie had also decided that she would try to help Austin whilst she was around. She wanted to help anybody that had grown up with Arnold Harrington. Life at the Harrington household was not a place where happiness could foster.

CHAPTER FIVE

Katie and Prue returned to the manor, both giggling and laden down with bags. After their heart-to-heart in the coffee shop, they had reminisced about the fun they had together in Brighton. Katie yearned for those days again but she could see on Prue's face that she had moved on and her life had changed. It surprised Katie as she felt a pang of envy. They had always been so different that neither of the women had ever compared their lives and jealousy had never come between them. As they continued to chat the feeling slowly eased and Katie felt herself relax back into Prue's company. After the coffee shop, they had popped into a few more shops as Prue remembered that they were having people over for dinner and they needed gin and potatoes.

"Did you girls have a good day?" Elliot asked, walking through from the kitchen.

"It was wonderful." Prue smiled back, holding the bag containing her wedding dress out of sight. Katie watched as Elliot embraced Prue - they looked so right together.

Elliot stepped back from the embrace and glanced at his watch. "Everyone will be round in an hour, do you want me to make a start on dinner?"

"Yes, please. We have to get ready!" Prue was almost bouncing up and down at the idea of getting ready, whereas Katie was grimacing.

"Elliot, would you like some help with cooking?" Katie tried to make her voice sound innocent and as though she really did want to help Elliot cook.

"You're not going anywhere. Come on, we have clothes to pick!" Prue grabbed Katie's hand and led her towards the stairs.

"Have fun, girls!" Elliot called after them, laughing to himself as he made his way towards the kitchen.

"I'll be kind, you can pick your own outfit." Prue smiled sweetly at Katie before disappearing into her own bedroom. Katie was left feeling nervous. Why was Prue being so casual about her outfit? With a sigh, Katie gave up trying to decipher the inner workings of her friend's brain and went to get ready.

The suitcase was still lying open on the floor, its contents mostly creased and so Katie's options were somewhat limited. She pulled out a pair of tartan skinny jeans, an ode to her Scottish heritage, and a green jumper. It wasn't fancy, nor was it something Prue would approve of but it was Katie and so that was what Katie would wear. Once dressed she ran some products through her hair to emphasise the curls. The falling snow had somewhat flattened her wayward curls. Although, that was not necessarily a bad thing. Katie was ready in a matter of minutes and so she made her way to Prue's bedroom.

Katie knocked on the bedroom door. "Come in!" Prue called from the other side. As Katie stepped inside the smell of perfume overwhelmed her, she tried to stop herself from coughing as it hit the back of her throat. Once Katie's senses had adjusted to the room her eyes fell upon Prue, sat at her dressing table. She was dressed in a beautiful silk burnt orange tea dress. It was simple and timeless, just like Prue herself. There was a part of Katie that yearned to be as stylish as Prue and yet she was also perfectly content with her own style.

"How's this?" Katie asked, giving Prue a little twirl.

"It's very you. Katie, when everyone gets here would you do drinks while I chat to Elliot? I want to talk to him about Austin, our chat today made me realise that we have to do what's best for him and forget about Arnold." Prue was worried about Arnold spreading hate against her, again.

Katie put her hand on Prue's shoulder, "you'll do the right thing Prue, you always do."

Half an hour later, their three guests stood in the hallway. Robert and Maggie looked very happy together. They had only recently made their relationship official but everyone had seen it blossoming for a while now. It was heartwarming to see two broken people come together, heal each other and find happiness. Austin stood to the side, looking as awkward as Katie felt. Meanwhile, Prue and Elliot were the centre of attention, enjoying playing host to their guests.

"Let's go straight into the dining room." Everyone followed Prue to the back of the house where the formal dining room was situated. Katie had only been in there once and since then, Prue had worked her magic on the room. It was a combination of modern and Art Deco, and it was beautiful. In the middle of the room sat a long mahogany table with sapphire coloured scalloped chairs surrounding it. The walls were adorned with navy wallpaper, covered in a geometric golden 1920s pattern. In the centre of the back wall sat a large sideboard, coated in gold leaf. Bottles of various liquors and fancy glasses sat on top of the sideboard, gleaming under the light that the chandelier cast upon them. At the end of the long room were French doors, leading out to the garden, but that wasn't what had caught Katie's attention. A second Christmas tree stood in front of the doors and was breathtaking. Covered in blue and gold baubles and twinkling lights, it was tastefully decorated, yet it felt just as festive as the tacky tree that Katie remembered from her childhood.

"Katie, will you get everyone drinks whilst I help Elliot with dinner?" Prue didn't wait for an answer before she made her way out of the dining room.

Katie glanced nervously around the room, although she knew these people they were still as good as strangers to her. A shyness crept up over her and she felt herself feeling more and more awkward. Robert and Maggie were talking to each other, and it was as though nobody else was in the room with them. Austin was stood only a few paces from Katie, looking as awkward as she felt.

"So, drinks?" Austin gave her a tentative smile as he pointed towards the sideboard that was heaving with alcohol.

"Yes! What would you like?" Katie was grateful for the icebreaker and immediately set about finding glasses. It was good to have something to focus on rather than trying not to stare at the stupidly handsome man stood next to her. Katie hadn't failed to notice how similar they had dressed;

Austin had on black skinny jeans and a green jumper. They were almost matching, if you didn't count the splash of tartan.

Austin began casting his eyes over the bottles. "Whatever has the lowest alcohol content, I've got to be up early."

Katie laughed and helped him to search through the bottles. "What about a gin and tonic but I'll pour you a half measure?" Austin nodded in reply and Katie busied herself preparing the drink. There was a bucket of ice at one end of the sideboard, Prue really had thought of everything.

"Which garnish would you like, sir?" Katie teased as she pointed to a plate filled with various garnishes ranging from a simple slice of lemon to grapefruit curls.

"Whatever is the most manly," he joked, winking at her.

"I believe that these are all considered 'manly'." Katie raised her brow back at him, enjoying the effortless banter between the two of them.

"Good point! I've spent far too much time around my father. I'm going to assert my independence and have a slice of cucumber."

Katie couldn't help but laugh as she watched Austin pick up the slimy piece of cucumber, which quickly fell out of his grip and 'plopped' rather unceremoniously in his glass. It was a relief to find that his views did not echo those of his father.

"I think I might just opt for a wedge of lime." Katie poured her own drink and took a big sip. She wasn't a big drinker, but she felt in need of some liquid courage to get through tonight. Her shy persona was not suited to gatherings like this. On nights out with Zac, she would shrink into the background and nobody would pay any attention to her. Tonight, Katie strongly suspected that Prue would ensure that she felt included all evening.

"Shall I take orders?" Austin asked. He must have seen the expression on Katie's face as she tried to muster up the courage to approach Robert and Maggie.

Katie stood by the sideboard, trying to make herself look busy as Austin approached his mother and Robert to ask them what drinks they wanted. A small part of Katie was angry at herself. She was in such beautiful surroundings with such lovely people, so why couldn't she just relax and enjoy everyone's company? She doubted herself. Why would anyone want to spend time with her?

Austin returned, making Katie jump, "Robert would like a strong G and T, like father like daughter, and mum would like a glass of sherry. Apparently, Prue's great-aunt, Carol is coming so you might as well pour a sherry for her, too." Katie's hands shook slightly as she prepared the drinks, another person joining their party set her nerves on edge. Prue was the social butterfly, whilst Katie was the creative introvert.

"Katie, I know we've barely spoken, but can I ask you a huge favour?" Austin had turned his full attention on her and was beaming at her. Katie had to put down the bottle of sherry as her hands shook. What was he about to say?

"Would you come Christmas shopping with me tomorrow afternoon? I need some help; Prue's too busy with wedding plans and I cannot ask my mother to choose her own present." Austin held his breath as he waited for a reply. He looked as nervous as Katie felt. Katie let out a sigh of relief. As nerve-racking as an afternoon with Austin would be, at least they would have something to distract them.

"I'd love to, I have a couple more presents I need to buy."

"Thank you! I have everyone to buy for." Austin blushed slightly at his confession, Katie laughed and rolled her eyes. They would definitely have a distraction.

"Elliot's just gone to get Carol," Prue announced as she walked into the room. Katie handed her a drink and followed her to the table where she sat down opposite Maggie. Austin chose the seat next to her.

"Katie, we haven't had a chance to catch up yet." Maggie smiled sweetly across the table at her. She looked much happier than she had during Katie's last visit to Ivy Hatch. Her eyes glistened with happiness and Katie couldn't help but notice Robert holding her hand. They looked very content together.

"I've barely sat down since I arrived!" Katie giggled, the gin was slowly easing her inhibitions.

"Prue, give the girl a break!" Robert chuckled as he gave his daughter a loving smile. Katie couldn't help but feel as though she were intruding on a private moment. A part of her wished her own father were there to tell her everything would be okay but he was thousands of miles away working in America.

"I've got to work tomorrow, so she has a break. Unless you want to come to work with me?" Prue smiled sweetly. Katie knew that Prue was referring to her earlier offer of a job. She didn't know what to say but thankfully she didn't need to as Austin spoke up.

"Actually, Katie's coming Christmas shopping with me tomorrow." The entire room erupted into laughter at Katie's expense.

"You're brave!" Maggie exclaimed, a soft smile on her face as she glanced over at her son.

Katie continued to sip at her gin and felt herself relax into her surroundings. She soon felt okay with everyone in the room. Carol had arrived and greeted everyone with a big hug and Katie immediately felt at ease. Perhaps one day she might be half as social as Prue. Sitting next to Austin had been Prue's genius plan but Katie couldn't be angry at her, she had a brilliant time talking to Austin. Katie couldn't help but feel herself starting to fall for him, she had to be careful. Everybody knew Katie had a tendency to fall for the wrong type and once she started she fell quickly.

CHAPTER SIX

Austin had been busy at the farm all morning and so Katie had a relaxing morning on her own at the manor. Both Prue and Elliot had left early for work, leaving Katie to enjoy her surroundings in peace. She made a cup of tea, treated herself to an extra sugar and went to sit in the library. As Katie sat looking at the books surrounding her, she thought about her mother, who was an avid reader. Her parents had separated when Katie was young; her father flew off to America for work whilst her mother flitted around, often leaving Katie in the care of distant aunts. It had been a chaotic upbringing. Katie had been left trying to find her place in the world and a place to call home. To her surprise, Ivy Hatch seemed to be the place she had been searching for.

With her cup of tea in hand and a blanket over her legs, Katie picked up one of the many books on the coffee table and began reading. There was nothing she loved more than a good book. She had even illustrated a few books over the last year.

A couple of hours later and Katie had finished her book. Her cup of tea sat on the table, cold and forgotten as the story had captured her attention. It had been ages since Katie had sat and read a book in one go, usually she was too busy with work or trying to please her idiot of an ex. Now she had spare time to read and she was enjoying it. The grandfather clock in the corner began to chime and Katie realised that it was already midday. She only had half an hour until Austin picked her up for their shopping trip. With a shriek of nerves and excitement she jumped up and made her way up to her bedroom, wondering what to wear. She was slowly turning into Prue.

With some panic, Katie opted for black skinny jeans, a black roll neck, black Dr Martens and a long, slightly oversized, green coat. It was simple and yet stylish; she hoped. There was no time to properly tame her hair and so Katie piled it on top of her hair in a messy bun. It looked as though she had just rolled out of bed and thrown it on top of her head, which rather accurately described it. Katie glanced at her sparse collection of make-up but decided against it, she was helping Prue's brother-in-law buy his Christmas presents. It wasn't a date.

Katie grabbed her bag as she heard the rumble of an engine coming up the driveway. Nerves were furiously bubbling away in the pit of her stomach but she did her best to control them. Austin was no longer a stranger, and she was only going shopping with him. It would be fine. At least, she hoped it would be. The snow had stopped falling today, however there was still a white dusting covering everything in sight.

"Hello!" Austin called as Katie made her way over towards the car, careful not to slip on the icy ground. It was freezing out and Katie wished she had opted for a hat.

"Afternoon." Katie smiled as she jumped into the passenger seat of the car, she was very grateful to discover that the heating had been on.

"Thank you for giving up your afternoon and helping me. I really wouldn't have known where to start without you." Austin shot Katie a smile before he turned the car around and made his way back down the driveway. Katie had to stop herself from letting out a girlish giggle at the mere sight of his smile. She really would need to get a grip on herself if she was to spend all afternoon with him. Katie reminded herself that she was here to help Austin do his Christmas shopping, not to flirt with him.

"I had nothing else to do." Katie shrugged off his compliment. It took all of her resolve not to keep staring at him. His dark hair was growing wild and flopped across his head, he had to keep pushing it back as it got in his eyes. His dark blue eyes were focused on the road ahead, something Katie was very grateful for, she knew for sure that her no-flirting rule would be decimated if his eyes were on her. A side-effect of her shy nature was verbal diarrhoea, however it presented itself in the form of unprecedented flirting. Austin's good looks, the smattering of stubble around his jawline and his charming smile were a dangerous combination. Who knew what might tumble out of Katie's mouth? For this reason, Katie was always silent around Zac's friends. He would not have appreciated her awkward flirting with his friends.

"So, who do you have to buy for?" Katie asked, trying to stop her mind from whirring. Austin Harrington was far too attractive for his own good. They would get nothing done if Katie couldn't stop admiring him.

"Katie, I wasn't joking when I said I have everyone to buy for. Although, perhaps we can cross my father off that list." The tone of Austin's voice transformed as he mentioned his father. Katie hadn't met Arnold Harrington, however she had heard enough about him to know that she never wanted to make his acquaintance. Katie didn't really know what to say, but she felt as though she had to fill the silence.

"Do you want to talk about it?" Katie's voice was a whisper, she wasn't sure whether it was the right thing to say. It was one of those rare moments when she wished she was more like Prue; Prue would have known what to say to Austin.

"I'm not sure, Katie. I feel like I need to talk to somebody but I've only just met you." He sounded unsure of himself.

"Tell me." Katie replied, reaching out to brush her hand against his, which was perched on top of the gear stick.

"I've been an idiot, Katie and I've treated people terribly. I always knew my father's views were wrong, but I supported him because he was my father. Once I saw Elliot and my mother move away, I realised just how much he was controlling my life. I want to modernise the farm and look towards my future but he won't let me. The animals are suffering because of it and it breaks my heart to have to stand back and watch." Austin sighed as he finished his explanation. Katie felt her heart ache for him, he had been trying to do the right thing by his father but he was suffering for it.

"Prue and Elliot have offered you your own farm, haven't they?"

Austin nodded his head, "yes, they have. I feel guilty for leaving my other brother."

"I think it's time you started working towards your own

happiness, there'll come a time when your brother has to make his own decisions."

"Katie, that is probably the most sensible thing anyone has said to me." He shot her another one of those smiles and Katie felt her heart hammer in her chest.

They lapped into a comfortable silence for the remainder of the journey. Katie tried to busy her mind by thinking who else she had to buy Christmas presents for. She had everything, but she still needed to buy Prue and Elliot a wedding present.

"Who are we shopping for first and what's your budget?" Katie asked as Austin parked the car and turned the engine off. They were in the same town that Prue had taken Katie to for their dress shopping.

"Let's do my mum and Prue, first. I think they're the two I'll need the most help with. The budget is negotiable, I've been doing some consultancy work for a few farms in the area, helping them to modernise their approaches." Austin climbed out of the car, leaving Katie staring after him in awe. She shook her head and forced herself to climb out of the car. There would be plenty of time to swoon over Austin once she was back at the manor, alone.

Once outside the car, Katie couldn't help but notice they were almost matching, again. A smile crossed her face as she saw he was still wearing his green farmer wellies. You could take the man away from the farm but he would always be a farmer.

Katie led Austin to an antique shop that she had noticed whilst shopping with Prue. Prue had looked in longingly at a tea set and Katie had decided to buy it for their wedding present. It might not have been Elliot's dream present, but hey, happy wife, happy life!

"Do you think Prue would like this?" Austin called Katie over, he was stood by the jewellery section. Katie gasped as she saw what Austin was pointing at, it was the most beautiful pair of Art Deco drop earrings. A diamond halo surrounded a stunning emerald. They were breathtaking.

"They're absolutely beautiful," Katie replied. She couldn't take her eyes off of them. In that moment she felt very jealous of Prue opening her gift on Christmas morning.

"I think they're a maybe." Austin's eyes shone as he realised he had chosen a winner all by himself.

They spent the next few hours shopping and slowly ticking everyone off of Austin's list. The only person he had left now was his father but he told Katie he would get something on his own.

"Shall we grab a coffee before we head back?" Katie clasped a hand to her mouth as the words tumbled out of their own accord. She had been thinking about asking Austin for a coffee. She had never meant to actually say it out loud. What if he said no?

"Yes, please." The snow was falling again and so they quickly crossed the street and breathed a sigh of relief as they became ensconced in the warm, welcoming cafe.

A waitress wandered over to their table before Katie had even had time to take her coat off.
"What can I get you two?"

"Could I have a hot chocolate please, with cream?" Technically, she was on holiday and everybody knew that holiday calories didn't count.

"Could I have the same, please?" Austin smiled up at the waitress and Katie narrowed her eyes as she watched the woman swoon under his attention.

"Do you drink coffee?" Austin asked, once the waitress had finally pulled her gaze away from him and returned to the counter to prepare their drinks.

"I hate the stuff. What about you? I would have thought you lived it on it with your early mornings."

"I can't stand the stuff either." A look passed between the two of them, their eyes lingering on one another for a little longer than necessary.

"So Katie, you know I'm a lowly farmer who's scared of his own father, now I want to know about you."

"There's not much to know. I'm currently homeless and jobless." Katie shrugged her shoulders and stared down at the lace tablecloth in front of her. She wished she hadn't told Austin that.

"That sounds tough. If you ever need someone to chat to, I'm here." He smiled at her, not that charming, heart pounding smile; this one was gentle and full of concern. It almost made her heart explode.

Austin quickly took her mind off of her own woes and distracted her with anecdotes of farm life. Katie confessed that she knew a little more about farm life than she liked to admit, she had spent many years of her childhood on her grandfather's farm. She didn't stop laughing all afternoon. Katie and Austin were lost in their own little bubble, getting to know one another. It came as quite a shock to them when they tore themselves from each other's eyes to see that it was now dark outside.

"We better head home before Prue sends out a search team for us." Reluctantly, they made their way back to the manor, neither of them uttering a word in fear of bursting their little bubble.

CHAPTER SEVEN

The manor was silent, after all it was only 5am. Katie threw on a jumper over her leggings and made her way down to the kitchen to make a cup of tea. She had always been an early riser and being in Ivy Hatch had not changed that. She was enjoying making a cup of tea and watching as the village awoke in the distance. Katie could see the Christmas Tree from its position on the village green, its lights were twinkling.

"You got home late with Austin." Katie jumped, splashing herself with water as she filled the kettle at the sink. She spun around to see Prue sat at the breakfast bar, in her silk dressing gown sipping black coffee.

"We had a lot of shopping to do." Katie shrugged her shoulders and turned back to the kettle. She didn't want Prue to see the blush rising on her cheeks at the mention of Austin. They had a wonderful afternoon together, and he had dropped her off at the front door, dropping a kiss on her cheek.

"Is that code for something else?" Prue wiggled her eyebrows. Katie groaned at her teasing, she needed at least one cup of tea inside of her before she could cope with Prue's incessant teasing.

"Leave me alone to drink my tea." Katie smiled at Prue so

she knew she was joking. Well, mostly joking.

"Fine! Can I ask you a favour?" As Katie took a closer look she realised Prue looked very stressed.

"Of course, what's wrong?"

"I've got to go into work today, at the auction house, but I'm supposed to be covering Maggie in the bookshop. Her and dad have gone away for the day as a pre-Christmas treat." Prue sighed, tugging a hand through her bed hair. Katie was not accustomed to seeing her best friend looking so unnerved.

"I'll cover the shop, it's fine. Besides, I need something to add to my CV." Despite the joke Katie felt her stomach twist as she remembered her unemployed status.

"Katie, there's always a job for you here, you know that."

"Thank you, Prue, I really appreciate it. Now, can I help you with any of your other stresses?" Katie took her tea and sat down next to Prue, putting an arm around her shoulders.

"I'll be fine, I'm just trying to juggle too many things at the moment," she sighed and downed the dregs of her coffee. "I've got to go and get ready, we've got an early delivery and I have to open up at the auction house. Call me if you need anything at the bookshop."

Katie promised Prue that she would be okay and went back to drinking her cup of tea, spinning round on her chair so that she could see the village at the bottom of the hill. She couldn't help it as her eyes sought out the Harrington's farm. Austin would be down there - probably out in the fields already. Her dreams had been filled with a certain someone's indigo eyes.

As Katie went upstairs to get ready for the day ahead, she realised she would have to walk into the village as both Prue and Elliot had already left for the day. Somehow, it was still snowing outside. With a sigh, Katie got dressed for the day in a grey jumper and another pair of black jeans. She pulled a hat on over her unruly hair and stashed a few hairbands in her pocket; it was going to be a job to tame her mane once she got inside the shop.

The walk down to the shop was almost enjoyable, at least it would have been without the icy wind that kept whipping around Katie's legs. She had to concentrate on her footing down the steep hills, in fear of slipping and sliding down them. That was all she needed. As she got closer to the bookshop, she felt a little bubble of happiness within her. Nobody could be in a foul mood inside the bookshop. She passed the little craft shop and stared in, longingly. Hours could be spent within those four walls spending an enormous sum of money. Thankfully, Katie had packed her sketch pad to ease herself back into her creative pursuits.

Katie unlocked the door and stepped inside *The Vintage Bookshop of Memories*, careful not to let any snow blow in with her. She stood on the mat and took off her many layers, hanging them up by the door. Her mind wandered back to a few days ago when she stepped through this door. In such a short time, she already felt so much happier and in charge of her life again. There really was something magical about this village - it manifested happiness. Despite, Prue's icy reception when she returned, everyone had now accepted the Clemonte presence in the village. Prue had brought about equality and with that Ivy Hatch had blossomed.

After making herself a cup of Tea, Katie put the 'open' sign outside the shop, the same one that she had designed. As she walked back to the stool behind the antique cash register, she brushed past a shelf of books, causing a book to fall to the floor. As Katie leant down to pick it up, she realised it was one of her favourites, *Beauty and the Beast*. She picked it up and took it over to her seat, taking a sip of tea before opening it. She could lose herself in the book for an hour or two before she got on with anything productive. As Katie opened the book a piece of paper floated out, landing on her lap. It was one of the notorious notes which were found ensconced within the pages. Katie unfolded the paper and stared down at the three words in front of her. *Follow your heart.*

"Utter nonsense," Katie muttered to herself, placing the note back inside the book and returning it to the shelf. She would not be drawn in by cute notes hidden in books. Her heart was a fortress and there would be no following it. Having given up on the idea of reading Katie pulled the sketch pad out of her backpack and decided to doodle. Her creative endeavours were her only source of income now and so she wanted to exercise her creativity.

The morning passed relatively quickly with a few people popping in for books. It was still snowing outside, each person who stepped into the bookshop breathed a sigh of relief as the warmth wrapped around them and they found themselves in a book-lover's heaven. Katie busied herself sketching the interior of the shop, in-between helping customers find the perfect books for Christmas presents. After finishing another sketch of the Bookshop, Katie turned over to a fresh page and sketched Austin from memory. To her surprise, she could remember everything about his face, even those three little worry lines in the middle of his forehead. His eyes glistened back at her as she looked down at her creation - even she was amazed at the likeness.

"Not bad but I think my jaw is a little more chiselled." Katie jumped as she became aware of someone looming over her shoulder, looking down at the sketch pad in her lap. A blush rose on her cheeks as she realised it was Austin and he'd just caught her sketching him from memory. She hadn't missed a single detail, which was either incredibly embarrassing or a credit to her creativity.

"It was just a quick doodle." She brushed off his comment and placed the sketch pad down on the counter, facing downwards.

"Sorry, I didn't mean to embarrass you," he teased. The blush on her cheeks was only deepening and Katie knew there nothing she could do or say to lessen it.

"It's your fault for being so sketch-able." Katie hadn't meant to encourage him but it had slipped out before she could stop herself.

"I'm going to take that as a compliment. Anyway, I saw Prue on my rounds and she mentioned that you were working here today and said you might not have time to get some lunch. So, here I am, your knight in shining armour."

Katie had to stop herself from rolling her eyes. Of course Prue would set her up with Austin like this. Her friend knew her far too well. She also probably knew that Katie's social awkwardness combined with her flirty nature would end up in her encouraging Austin. She sighed; there were worse things she could be doing during her festive break.

"Thank you, Austin." She smiled at him, a genuine smile. She really was grateful that he had taken the time to bring her something to eat.

"I'm on my lunch break, too, so I thought we could eat together, if that's okay?" That was more than okay. Katie had to stop herself before the words trundled out of her mouth. There was leading him on and then there was being too forward. It was a tricky balance to strike, especially when you suffered from verbal diarrhoea.

"Are you okay?" Austin asked her, watching as Katie's mind whirled.

"Fine, sorry! So what are we feasting on?" Katie focused on the man in front of her. Despite being on his lunch break she suspected he had popped back to the farm to change. She wondered whether that was for her benefit or if he just smelled of farm life.

"I've brought sandwiches and hot chocolate. You should be happy to know that they both came from the cafe, I'm not much of a cook."

"You don't have to be much of a cook to make a sandwich!"

"You grossly underestimate sandwich making." Katie shook her head and laughed at Austin's response, she supposed he had always been busy on the farm, not in the kitchen learning from Maggie. For someone that had such an old-fashioned upbringing they were very similar.

Austin pulled up a stool next to Katie and they both bit into their sandwiches, silence enveloping them as they enjoyed their well-earned lunch.

"It's only five days until the wedding!" Austin broke the silence.

"I know. Prue looked particularly stressed this morning."

"Don't mention anything but her and Elliot had an argument. She thinks he should invite our father, but he won't hear of it." Austin's own face looked conflicted.

"What do you think?" Katie wanted to know Austin's opinion. Prue was too quick to forgive and to try to mend bridges.

"I think she should give up trying to include him in any of our lives. I've signed the contract for the new farm, I'm moving in over the new year." Without thinking Katie threw her arms around him, she was so happy for him. Austin froze as her arms wrapped around him and for a horrible moment Katie thought she had done the wrong thing. Then he relaxed into her embrace.

"I'm so happy for you," Katie murmured, pulling away from Austin and feeling slightly embarrassed at her rash actions.

"Thank you, Katie. It means a lot." He smiled at her, before reaching over to grab the flask of hot chocolate and pouring them each a mug. Just like that the moment had passed, they were back to being friends. However, nobody could wipe the memory of that embrace from Katie's mind.

They drank their hot chocolate and chatted for a bit. The smile didn't leave Katie's face once, the entire time Austin was there next to her she was beaming. There was just something about his presence that filled her with joy. He brought out the happiness within her and that was something she had been searching for, for a long time. It was silly though; he was a farmer from a little village, miles away from her hometown of Brighton. Although, could Katie still call Brighton her hometown since she no longer had a home there? She didn't actually have a home anywhere. She was a stray and thankfully Prue had taken pity on her but she couldn't stay for much longer. Prue and Elliot would soon be married, and they needed their space.

"You're nothing like your father." Katie wanted to take the words back as soon as they had tumbled from her mouth. What an awful thing to say.

"My father didn't really bring us up, he was always out on the farm. He taught me some of it but the rest I taught myself. I was either on the farm or reading with my mother. The only time I really saw my father was when we all had to sit together for dinner. As I got older, we spent more time together as he taught me more and more on the farm. By then I already knew his view on life was wrong. We clash a lot." There was a deep-rooted sadness behind Austin's beautiful eyes. Katie wanted nothing more than to throw her arms around him again but one impromptu hug was enough for today.

"I'm sorry," she whispered, opting to reach out and squeeze his hand, instead. There was something so perfect about the feel of his skin on hers, like it was meant to be. Katie sighed, there she was getting all soppy again. He was just a man, a very good-looking man, who happened to be in her life at this moment in time but who knew where they'd both be in a month's time.

"Katie, will you go out with me tomorrow evening?" Austin's usual confident persona had faded, instead he looked down at her hand still gripping his. His eyes were filled with nerves. Katie considered how well she could read him - his eyes really were windows to his soul.

For a brief moment, Katie was speechless. Not something that happened easily, usually the worst case-scenario was that she blurted out something completely unrelated. However, today she just sat blinking back at Austin, as her brain refused to conjure up any words.

"Sorry, I shouldn't have asked." Austin looked embarrassed as he stood up and quickly gathered the remnants of their lunch.

"No, I'm sorry, you just caught me by surprise. I'd love to go out with you tomorrow evening." Katie breathed a sigh of relief as her brain finally began to function again and her ability to speak returned.

"Are you sure? Please don't say yes out of pity." If anyone deserved pity, it was her. Katie didn't say that out loud.

"Austin, I want to go out with you." She smiled at him, putting her own woes to the back of her mind. She would do everything she could to enjoy the short time she had in Ivy Hatch, after-all, who knew what direction her life was about to take?

"Good. I'll pick you up from the manor at about 5! See you."

Katie waved after him, she'd lost the ability to speak again. She had a date with Austin Harrington. That had not been a part of her plans. Was it stupid to go on a date with someone when she'd be leaving soon? Although, there was nothing stopping her from making a new life here in Ivy Hatch. Could she see herself becoming a farmer's wife? Katie blushed, where had that thought come from? One date and she was already considering marrying the man. No, her life was back in Brighton. She could have some fun with Austin but she couldn't fall for him. It was simple - just have fun, don't catch feelings. Simple.

CHAPTER EIGHT

"Four more days!" Elliot announced as he wandered into the kitchen where Prue and Katie sat sharing some toast. The weather outside made Katie want to wrap herself up in a blanket and spend the day in-front of the television, watching Christmas films. However, Prue had other plans.

"I know. We're off to do some wedding bits today." Prue smiled up at her husband-to-be.

"Make sure you get Katie back with enough time to get ready for her date this evening." Katie could have thrown her buttery slice of toast at Elliot's head. So far she had got away without Prue asking how her lunch with Austin had gone.

"A date?!" Prue cried out in amazement. Elliot held his hands up and muttered an apology to Katie.

"It's not exactly a date. Austin just asked me out this evening." Katie shrugged, staring down at her toast as if it were the most interesting thing she had ever laid her eyes upon.

"We need to buy you a new outfit. What are you doing?"

"I'm not sure." Katie winced and held her breath, waiting for Prue's reply.

"Well, what did he tell you to wear?"

"Umm, he didn't say, and I didn't ask." Katie saw Elliot snigger from where he stood by the kettle. They both knew that Prue would not be happy to hear this.

"You didn't ask?" This time Prue was shouting and Katie recoiled from the noise. How could somebody get so animated about clothes?

"Prue, it's my date, not yours. I'll sort an outfit later." Katie didn't know where that rush of confidence had come from, but she had enjoyed it.

"Sorry, I didn't mean to overreact like that. Wedding stress is not helping matters." Prue sighed and placed her head in her hands. Katie was beginning to worry about her best friend, she had lost her spark.

"What's wrong, Prue?" Katie leant across the table to hold Prue's hand, from the corner of her eye she could see Elliot glancing over in concern.

"I'm just trying to juggle too much. Yesterday, the only craft shop in the village gave me notice that they're looking to move out." Prue sighed. Katie's mind began racing.

Craft shop.

"Prue, you really must be stressed." Katie giggled, Prue really had missed out on the perfect opportunity.

"What?" Prue asked, looking over at Katie, her perfect complexion was spoilt by worry lines in the middle of her forehead.

"A craft shop. What am I amazing at?" It took Prue a moment to realise what Katie was saying.

"Do you want the craft shop?" Both women were almost bouncing up and down in excitement at the prospect.

"Why don't we call it a trial? I've got nothing else to do so I may as well try it!"

"Oh Katie, this is perfect. I can't believe you're going to be staying." Prue jumped up and came round to the other side of the table to throw her arms around her friend.

"I just need to find somewhere to live." Katie hugged her friend back. She really was grateful for having such an amazing woman in her life.

"You can stay here for as long as you want." Prue was sincere in her offer, but Katie didn't want to take advantage.

"What are you two actually up to today?" Elliot asked. The kettle had finally boiled, and so he had his coffee in hand as he took a seat at the table with them.

"We've got to go and check the flowers, then pick up the suits and the wedding favours. What are you up to today?"

Katie zoned out as Elliot told Prue about his day ahead of him. Lucky Elliot got to go to work whilst Katie would be dragged around the shops doing some '*wedmin*' as Prue had referred to it.

The day passed in a blur of wedding-related activities. Prue was so busy worrying about all the details that she didn't have time to quiz Katie on her upcoming date. Despite being dragged around shops Katie couldn't help but smile, her future was beginning to come together. She could run the craft shop and indulge in her own creative pursuits. Perhaps she could even talk to Prue about selling her own pictures in the shop. The possibilities were endless. Not to mention the date that she had that evening.

Once home, Katie slipped upstairs to jump in the shower, she only had an hour until Austin would be there and she didn't want to rush. Thankfully, Prue was busy hanging up all the suits that they had collected and so she didn't notice Katie's disappearance.

As Katie made her way back out of the bathroom and into her bedroom, she jumped as she saw Prue sat on her bed.

"You didn't think I'd give up that easily, did you?" She joked, holding a parcel on her lap, wrapped in festive paper.

"I'm not dressing up, Prue!" Usually, Katie would allow Prue to dress her, however this was different. Tonight she wanted to be herself and let Austin get to know her. That included getting to know her 'jeans and a jumper' winter style.

"I'm not going to choose your outfit for you. Although, I wanted to give you your Christmas present early in case it's something you might want to wear."

Katie rolled her eyes and sat down on the bed next to Prue. Slowly, she unwrapped the present; she knew it was clothing related, and she only hoped it was more her style than Prue's. Prue meant well but Katie would never suit the same clothes that she liked. Katie gasped as she removed the gift from the paper, her hand brushed against the most beautiful fabric. Prue had bought her a cream cashmere jumper with a big roll neck. It was comfortable and yet had a hint of style to it.

"Oh Prue, I love it!" Katie threw her arms around her friend, careful not to let her towel fall.

"Good! I'm learning Katie, I'm trying not to force you into liking the same things as I do."

After a few tears and another hug, Prue left Katie alone to get ready for her date. She left her hair to air dry whilst she pulled on a pair of black skinny jeans, paired with her beautiful new jumper. It was perfect. Katie then opted for a little bit of make-up, creating a smoky look on her eyes. Finally, she pulled on a pair of black boots with a slight heel and let her hair tumble down her back. She was finally ready for her date with Austin Harrington.

CHAPTER NINE

Katie felt like a teenager again as she heard a knock at the front door and somebody from downstairs opened it. She felt the butterflies swarm in her stomach, this date meant a lot to her and she wanted it to go well. It was her first date since her heart had been broken, if she was completely honest with herself, she was scared about tonight. What if she fell for him? Slowly, she made her way down the staircase, trying to rid her mind of the negative thoughts. As she saw Austin in the hallway talking with Elliot, she paused on the stairs, allowing herself a moment to take in Austin's appearance. His hair was as dishevelled as ever, Katie was beginning to realise that it was just his usual hairstyle. He was dressed in matching black skinny jeans, a grey jumper and a quilted Barbour coat. At least he wasn't wearing the wellington boots tonight. His eyes shone as he spoke to his brother. Katie had to stop herself from focusing on his eyes and forced herself to walk down the last few steps and make her presence known.

"Your lovely date for the evening, sir." Elliot teased, he had spent far too much time around Prue.

"Katie, you look lovely." Austin side stepped his brother and came to give Katie a peck on the cheek. It was polite but something about it made Katie's heart flutter. A sweet gesture that showed so much about his personality.

"Let me just grab a jacket and we'll go." Before Katie could walk more than two steps Prue threw a jacket into her arms and ushered her towards the door.

"Don't do anything we wouldn't!" Elliot shouted after them, chuckling to himself.

Katie got into the passenger side of Austin's car without uttering a word. She was mortified by their behaviour, at least Austin was familiar with Elliot and Prue's behaviour.

"Sorry about my brother." Austin apologised, starting the engine.

"Sorry about my best friend." They both laughed, at least they could see the funny side to the teasing.

"What are we doing this evening?" Katie asked, looking down at the jacket in her arms. It was Prue's, not hers. So much for not picking her outfit for her.

"There's a Christmas market over in one of the villages, I thought it might be nice to have a wander round and perhaps grab some dinner somewhere?" It sounded perfect to Katie.

"Is this just another sneaky way to get me to do your Christmas shopping for you?" Katie joked, smiling to herself as she saw a few stray snowflakes fall from the sky. It was a beautiful evening and in less than an hour the dark sky would be lit up with twinkling stars and the moon would cast shadows over the market.

They chatted about their day as the car trundled down the country lanes to one of the neighbouring villages. Katie let out a gasp as they pulled up. There was a tree in the middle of the village which towered over everything. It was beautifully adorned with red and golden decorations, all of which twinkled in the fairy lights wrapped around the tree. An enormous star sparkled at the top. It was beautiful. Tonight was worlds apart from her first date with Zac, who had brought her to a trendy wine bar for drinks. She had spent the whole night feeling like an outcast. This was different, Katie really felt like Austin understood her; she just didn't know whether she was ready to risk her heart again.

"The market is just down there." Austin pointed to a little cobbled side street, forcing Katie back into the present. Katie returned her attention to Austin and pulled on the jacket that Prue had given her. It wasn't until she climbed out of the car she realised it matched Austin's. She was going to empty all of Prue's bottles of gin, when she got home, and replace them all with water.

Austin took hold of her hand and led her towards the market. She told herself that he was just trying to keep their hands warm but Katie knew she wasn't fooling anyone. He was holding her hand because this was a date. The butterflies in her stomach began fluttering around again.

As they turned into the street, Katie gasped. The scene infront of her was breathtaking. The market was comprised of both little shops and wooden huts, all adorned with Christmas decorations. Snow lined the roofs and a few of the chimneys were smoking. It was like something from a Christmas card. A few people were wandering along, looking at the Christmas delights on offer but it was relatively quiet.

"This is my idea of heaven." Katie confessed as they walked

down the street. The shops ranged from handmade Christmas baubles, a sweet little chocolate shop selling handcrafted gingerbread truffles and even a small stall selling Christmas themed dog collars.

"Perhaps I should get one of these for my future sheep herder." Austin led them over to the dog collar stall. There were some cute designs.

"Perhaps get the dog first." Katie laughed, picking up a small green collar with little sausage dogs on it, each one wearing a bow tie covered in Christmas trees. She would buy it and send it to her mother, who would appreciate the gesture since she had recently acquired a little bundle of fur. It would also make Katie feel like her mother was a part of Christmas.

Christmas music played in the background as they made their way around the other stalls. Austin bought a bottle of ginger spiced rum for Robert as a Christmas present. It was clear where Prue had inherited her love for spirits from.

"Shall we find somewhere to get some dinner? The market is open until late so we can have another wander round after?" Katie nodded in agreement and Austin led her towards a little Italian restaurant in the next street. He still hadn't let go of her hand.

They chose a table near the window so that they could watch everybody come and go, although there were few people out this evening. After all, it was a cold, snowy evening, and most people were at home snuggled up on the sofa watching a Christmas film. The restaurant was as typically Italian as you could get nestled in a little village in the English countryside. The tables were covered in gingham table clothes, which clashed spectacularly with the Christmas decorations that adorned the walls and even the ceiling. There was no mistaking what time of year it was in this little eatery.

"This is adorable," Katie remarked, putting her menu down in front of her. It hadn't taken her long to decide what she wanted for dinner.

"Isn't it? Mum would bring us to the village every year to look around the market and then we'd come here for dinner as a treat." Austin's eyes lit up as he recalled his childhood memories. Katie couldn't help but slide her hand across the table and take his hand in hers.

"That sounds lovely. Your dad didn't go?" She hated ruining the happy atmosphere, but Katie was still trying to understand Austin's upbringing and his relationship with his dad. She had to ask these difficult questions.

"No, he was always too busy with the farm. Although, I suspect it was more because he felt that it wasn't a man's place to take the kids out for a Christmas treat." Katie rolled her eyes. She still couldn't believe how dated Arnold's views were. Maggie had done an amazing job raising her children and staying sane with Arnold for a husband.

"It's nice that your mother made the effort to make some lovely Christmas memories with you. I think I've only spent a handful of Christmases with my mum." Their conversation was interrupted as the waiter came over to take their order. They both opted for lasagna and a glass of red wine, the perfect combination.

"You didn't spend much time with your mother?" As soon as the waiter was out of earshot, Austin raised the question.

"No, she was too busy travelling the world. My father left when I was young and set up home in America. At university, Prue and I bonded over our childhoods. Whilst Prue was brought up by her grandmother, I was passed between different aunties. I don't regret it though, it was quite fun." Katie smiled to reassure Austin. Most people felt sorry for her at this point, but she didn't want their pity. She had really enjoyed getting to know her various aunties, and each one had taken the time to teach her a new skill.

The food came and it was every bit as delicious as Katie had hoped it would be. They continued to exchange childhood memories as the lights were switched off and candles were lit. Eventually, they reluctantly pulled on their coats and ambled back outside into the biting cold air. It was snowing a little heavier now, but not enough to put them off of a last wander around the market. Neither of them felt ready for the night to end.

They walked around the market again, hand in hand, stopping briefly to buy hot chocolates, which they then took to the town centre where the tree stood. The lights twinkled down on them as they sat on a bench, sipping the steaming liquid. Katie had opted for cream and marshmallows, whereas Austin had decided on whipped cream and a chocolate flake.

Katie couldn't help but laugh as Austin took a sip of his drink and pulled away with a blob of cream on his nose.

"What?" He asked, wiping around his mouth. He missed the blob on his nose.

"It's on your nose." Katie giggled and leaned in to wipe it

off, using the tissue that had been wrapped around her cup.

"Thank you," Austin whispered. Their faces were centimetres apart. Katie glanced up; hanging off of the tree, just above their heads, was a sprig of mistletoe. Austin noticed it at the same time.

"We can't deny such a tradition," he muttered before leaning forward and capturing her lips with his. The sound of Christmas music playing in the background faded away and Katie forgot that she was sat out in the snow. All she could think about was Austin and kissing him; he tasted of chocolate. It was the most romantic kiss that she could ever wish for, and it did not disappoint. Austin Harrington was a good kisser. However, throughout the entire evening, Katie couldn't shake off the feeling that she was doing the wrong thing. Her life was in pieces. She needed to focus on that, not dating the first charming man she met.

CHAPTER TEN

Memories of Katie's previous relationship plagued her dreams. She woke a handful of times throughout the night with tears streaming down her cheeks. How had she allowed him to treat her so awfully? Meeting Austin had made her realise how Zac should have treated her. One particular evening out kept seeping into her dreams. It was a few weeks before they broke up. It was also the night when Katie started to realise how controlling Zac was.

◆ ◆ ◆

Katie stared at her reflection in the mirror and sighed - she really didn't want to go out tonight, however Zac was insisting. They were going for dinner and drinks with some of his work friends; all of whom were as loud as Zac. Katie was an introvert, but Zac was always encouraging her to be more outgoing. He said he was trying to help her enjoy life, and so Katie always tried to make the effort in fear of appearing boring.

"You're not wearing that, are you?" Katie jumped as Zac entered the room. She turned back to look at her reflection in the mirror. She had thought her black dress suited her.

"What should I wear?" She asked, not wanting an argument tonight. They still hadn't discussed the argument they had last night. Zac had refused to eat the dinner Katie had cooked, saying it was burnt. It wasn't, it was cooked perfectly. Katie was

feeling exhausted - emotionally and physically. It had taken a considerable amount of concealer to hide the bags under her eyes. Lately, Zac had been picking at everything she did - nothing was right.

"Wear this." Zac pulled out a bright orange dress with a cut out middle. It was awful, but he had bought it for her birthday a few weeks ago. Katie had smiled, thanked him, and then buried it deep in the back of the wardrobe. It showed too much flesh and clashed with her hair. She just didn't feel comfortable in it.

"Okay." Katie took the dress from him and slipped it on. She wasn't in the mood for another argument. If she refused to wear it he would only sulk with her. Katie took a deep breath and reminded herself that Zac thought she looked good in the dress. That was all that mattered.

"You look gorgeous." Zac wrapped his arms around her and kissed her, and just like that Katie forgot about how he had behaved the previous evening.

The night was a disaster. Zac drank too much and became very loud. Katie, meanwhile, was left sat watching as their group became rowdier and rowdier. She felt like an outsider, looking in on someone else's life. This wasn't how she wanted to spend her evenings. She wanted to spend her evenings with Zac at home, however he was here, and so she was too. Zac was right, she was boring, all she had to do was keep pushing herself and soon she would enjoy it.

She didn't enjoy herself. Thankfully, it was soon over and she drove everyone home. Zac made many comments on her driving abilities. Katie gripped the wheel and told herself not to rise to it, he was only trying to help her improve her skill. Once home he ignored her, went straight to bed and was snoring within a few seconds. Katie had sat by the window, starting out at the sea wondering whether she was happy or if Zac had told her she was happy.

❖ ❖ ❖

Katie woke with more tears streaming down her face. How had she allowed Zac to treat her so awfully for so long? He had played with each and every one of her emotions for his own benefit; leaving Katie an emotional wreck, trying to find herself again. She was just beginning to find herself and recover from the emotional abuse. What had she been thinking going on a date with Austin? It was too soon; she was too broken.

"Morning, sleepyhead." Prue's voice was like spun sugar as she took in Katie's rumpled appearance.

"Morning." Katie sighed, she already knew from her friend's tone that she wanted the gossip from her date. After their kiss last night, Austin had taken Katie home, kissing her once again before walking her to the front door. Katie had walked up to her room with a huge smile across her face, careful to avoid Prue and Elliot, who were wrapping presents in the living room. She wanted the chance to relive her memories over and over before Prue grilled her. She'd laid in bed, tossing and turning as her head and her heart battled. She liked Austin, she liked him so much it scared her. Her life was in pieces and she was emotionally damaged - she needed time to heal. Katie suspected that her relationship with Zac had been emotionally abusive and controlling. She had been too in love with him to notice. She couldn't risk making the same mistake. She couldn't keep seeing Austin and allow herself to be so vulnerable. Her heart wasn't ready to open itself up again.

"Oh, come on," Prue pouted, "I need something to distract me from wedding plans."

"I really like him," Katie shrugged as she made herself a cup of tea, trying to decide how to begin the conversation with Prue.

"He really likes you, I can tell." Prue's smile couldn't get any bigger if she tried. Katie sat down opposite her and picked the almond croissant up from the plate in front, tearing it down the middle and picking at the pastry.

"I think I need to end it." Katie could barely believe the words that had come out of her mouth. Her date with Austin had been amazing, but she couldn't throw herself into this relationship. She'd lost everything after the break-up of her last one and here she was, trying to re-build her life again. She couldn't take such a big risk. Her mind was made up.

"Oh Katie, don't break your heart now just to avoid getting it broken later. Austin's a good man, I think he'd treat you well." Prue put down the bunting that she was sewing, another *wedmin* task, and turned her full attention to the conversation.

"I think the timing is wrong, Prue. I need to focus on piecing my life together again, not falling in love with the first man that's shown me any attention. Last night, I had lots of dreams...well, nightmares, really. I think Zac was emotionally abusive towards me." Katie felt a rush of relief as she said the words out loud. How had it taken her this long to realise what had happened?

"Oh, Katie. I never liked him." Prue came round to Katie's side of the table and wrapped her arms around her. "You're going to be okay, I'll always be here for you."

They sat in silence as Katie relaxed into Prue's embrace. Katie didn't know how to deal with the sudden realisation that Zac had treated her so awfully.

"Austin would never treat you like that." Prue broke the silence.

"I know." Katie wasn't just saying it to please Prue, she really did know that Austin was different - he would never treat her so dreadfully.

"Why don't you tell him you need some time? Don't just end things, Katie." Prue squeezed her hand before getting up to make another cup of tea and to give Katie a minute to think. Perhaps slowing things down would be a good idea. She could try to piece her life back together and then they could begin dating again. That made more sense, although that wouldn't stop Katie from getting her heart broken, however she strongly suspected that Austin was worth taking that risk for.

"I'll tell him we can't date, yet." Katie felt much better now that she had a plan, especially since that plan didn't include breaking up with Austin forever, just temporarily.

"When are you going to do it?" Prue asked. Katie looked at the table filled with bunting that needed to be strung together. She would go to Austin now and then fill her afternoon with the monotonous task and perhaps a gin, or five.

"I'm going to go now!" Katie declared, standing up from the kitchen table and marching towards the door.

"Are you going to go in your pyjamas?" Prue was laughing so much it took a minute for Katie to realise what she had said. She glanced down at herself and sighed as she realised she was still wearing her *Beauty and the Beast* pyjamas. Not the ideal attire to semi-dump someone in.

Five minutes later she was dressed in leggings, a baggy jumper and her hair was thrown up on top of her head in a messy bun.

"Do you want a lift?" Prue asked. She already had the car keys in her hand, ready to leave.

"No, thank you. I think the walk will do me good. Save some bunting for me!"

The walk was long, and it was cold, but it gave Katie enough time to decide what she was going to say to Austin. She was dreading every second of what was to come but she knew she had to do this for herself; she wasn't strong enough to juggle a new relationship whilst trying to sort her life out.

She walked up to the farm and wondered what to do next. Should she knock on the door? Or would Austin be out in the fields?

"You okay?" A voice boomed across the yard, making Katie jump and lose her footing, landing on her bum. She quickly brushed herself off and stood up as someone came towards her. He looked almost like Austin, only his hair was blonde and much better kept.

"I'm looking for Austin." She replied before he could make a remark on her tumble.

"Oh, you're the girl that's falling for him!" It appeared all three of the Harrington brothers had inherited an infuriating sense of humour.

"Is he here?" Katie asked, ignoring the joke he had made at her expense.

"He's over in the back field." It looked far away, but that would not stop Katie. She nodded her thanks and began the walk. The fields were filled with frozen snow and more was threatening to fall. It was a cold and punishing walk as the wind howled across the open field. Katie kept pushing herself to keep moving; she had to talk to Austin.

"Katie!" Austin called in amazement as he caught sight of her walking towards him. He was more equipped for the weather with his wellington boots on, Katie's own ankle boots had let in a tonne of snow already.

"Austin, I need to talk to you," she called back, picking up her speed.

"Why didn't you call me?" He asked her as they met halfway. She hadn't thought of that but it wasn't exactly something you said over the phone.

"I needed to talk to you, face-to-face." She watched as his face fell, the smile replaced by a grimace and the shine in his eyes disappeared, he already knew what she was implying.

"Katie, don't. I thought we had fun together." He was almost begging her, taking both of her hands in his.

"Austin, I'm not saying never, just not now. My life is a mess, and it's not the right time for me to be throwing myself into a new relationship. I've been treated terribly, I just need some time to be okay. I'm staying in Ivy Hatch, so perhaps once I've got myself back on my feet we could go for a drink?" A glimmer of hope crossed Austin's face at her words, but it wasn't enough to replace the dejected look.

"We're going to have to spend a lot of time together over the next few days," he commented, avoiding addressing her almost-break-up.

"Then let's spend those days together, as friends. Let's build a friendship whilst I'm re-building my life and then we can go from there." Katie took a deep breath to stop herself from crying in-front of him. She had to keep reminding herself why she was doing this. It was better for both of them if she fixed herself before they got together.

"Okay," he replied.

"Goodbye, Austin." Katie turned and began her walk back before he could say anything else. As soon as her back was turned to him she allowed the first tears to roll down her cheeks. It really was an 'it's not you, it's me' moment, and it was awful. Katie blamed herself for not being strong enough to throw herself into a new relationship, but what could she do? She couldn't just turn on her courage and allow herself to be vulnerable.

Katie cried the entire way home as the snow covered her. By the time she arrived back at the manor she was freezing cold, her hair was wet and her cheeks were thoroughly tear stained. Prue enveloped her in a hug as soon as she stepped through the front door.

"Come on, I've run you a bath." Prue led her upstairs and left her to warm up.

Katie laid in the bath, filled with lavender, thinking about what she had just done. She had been so happy yesterday and yet here she was today, heartbroken - the exact thing that she had been trying to avoid. What had she been thinking? She'd just made the biggest mistake of her life. At least she had an afternoon of sewing bunting to distract her. Katie let out a sob at the thought. She had to be strong. She couldn't ruin Prue's wedding because she was so awful at making her own decisions.

CHAPTER ELEVEN

"Two days!" Katie groaned as Prue's high-pitched voice echoed throughout her head. She'd drunk too many gin fizzes last night and had gone to bed early to forget the day's events. It was safe to say that Katie was having many regrets. She had been a coward ending things with Austin, and for what? She was heartbroken anyway, not because she loved him but because she had the potential to love him.

"Did you hear me?" Prue sighed, shaking Katie slightly. Katie was wishing she had opted to stay at a hotel rather than at the Clemonte Manor. Although, the closest hotel was probably an hour away.

"Sorry, my head's banging," Katie replied, sitting up in bed. She felt dreadful. The Christmas spirit combined with the upcoming wedding meant that there was a party atmosphere in the manor. Which had only resulted in too much alcohol being consumed.

"I've brought you some tablets and water." Katie smiled to herself. This was why she was staying at the Clemonte Manor. She took the tablets and drank the glass of water, knowing that she would need all the help she could get to cope with Prue's excitement today.

"I'll just jump in the shower and then we can enjoy the

day!" Katie mustered up the best smile she could. It was Prue's hen-do today, and they were going to have a fun, girly day.

"Wait, before you do that, are you really okay?"

"I will be." Katie smiled, she meant it, she would be okay. She'd been through worse than this, however there was something different about this time. There was something about Austin. Perhaps there was such a thing as soulmates. Katie shook her head. She couldn't think like that, especially not today.

"If you want to sneak off at any point, you know you can." Prue gave her a quick hug before leaving Katie to jump in the shower.

Usually, hen parties were filled with alcohol, dancing and potentially a male stripper at the end of the night. Prue's hen party was very different - especially since their party comprised of Prue, Katie, Elliot's mother and Prue's elderly great-aunt. Being so close to Christmas, Prue's friends from Brighton could not make the trip and so they had settled for a quiet day, instead. Maggie had arranged the daytime events and Katie had taken care of the evening.

"Prue, what should I wear?" Katie didn't know what they were doing, and she figured it was her friend's day. She may as well let her have all the fun. A squeal came from downstairs as Prue came running to her rescue. Knights in shining armour were so outdated, it was all about best friends in 1940s fashion these days. Prue walked straight past Katie and over to one of the guest rooms that she'd turned into a walk-in wardrobe.

"Here you go!" Prue emerged, holding a beautiful emerald

coloured, silk tea-dress. It matched perfectly with Prue's plum coloured one. The colour would look beautiful with Katie's flaming hair.

"Prue, why is this dress in my size?" Katie asked, taking it from her. She had to stop the smile that was threatening to cross her face. Of course her friend kept a selection of clothes in her size, just in case she one day decided she wanted to be *fashionable*.

"Oh, is it?" Prue asked, feigning ignorance. "Auntie Carol and Maggie will be here in forty minutes!" With that, Prue went bouncing back down the stairs, leaving Katie to get herself ready.

The dress fitted perfectly, but Katie had expected nothing less. Prue knew what she was doing. She popped on some concealer and mascara to mask her swollen eyes. Her hair tumbled down her back in ringlets. Katie was slowly realising that clothes were an ingenious way of cloaking how you really felt.

Maggie and Carol arrived just as Katie reached the bottom of the stairs. Prue went over to the door to let them in. They exchanged hugs and kisses as everyone said hello and professed their excitement for the day ahead. Katie was looking forward to the day. She hoped it would be a pleasant distraction from the mess that her own life was in.

"What's the plan?" Katie asked, neither her nor Prue knew what they were up to.

"You'll see, come on." Everyone followed Maggie out to her car and climbed in. Carol sat in the front with Maggie, whilst Katie and Prue climbed in the back.

"You okay?" Prue whispered, leaning across the car to give her friend's hand a squeeze.

"I'm fine, now stop worrying about me and enjoy your day!" Katie smiled back at her friend. She didn't want anything to ruin the next few days. Prue deserved every ounce of happiness that came her way, and Katie wouldn't let anything compromise that. Maggie drove them into Ivy Hatch, parking by the church. They then followed her over to the little cafe, The Honey Pot. As they reached the door, the sign announced that it was 'closed'. Ignoring the sign, Maggie pushed open the door and held it open for Prue and Katie to walk ahead.

They stepped inside The Honey Pot and Katie could barely believe her eyes; it was beautiful. Many of the tables had been pushed to the sides, leaving only one in the middle. The table was covered with a white lace cloth with a few vases of red roses scattered along it. There were two cake stands adorned with afternoon tea treats. Sandwiches, scones and the top tier was covered with Christmas delights. Miniature yule logs, a pistachio mousse pipped in the shape of a Christmas tree and miniature Christmas puddings. Above the table hung some bunting that Prue and Katie had been working on yesterday. Elliot must have taken some and given it to his mother. It was beautiful, and every inch screamed Prue. Katie had to take a deep breath to stop herself from crying; this time it was happy tears. She was happy to see how loved her friend was by the people of Ivy Hatch.

"Do you like it?" Wendy, the cafe owner, stepped out from behind the counter.

"Oh Wendy, it's beautiful." Prue threw her arms around the woman and Katie couldn't help but notice a stray tear make its way down her face. Wendy had been the first person to stand up for Prue when she came to Ivy Hatch, and so this must have meant a lot to her.

"Please, everyone sit down." Wendy gestured for them to each take a seat, then she turned back to the serving area, coming back with pots of tea.

"Are you joining us, Wendy?" Katie asked, unable to take her eyes off of the delights in front of her. In that moment, Katie realised how comfortable she felt around these women; Ivy Hatch was already changing her.

"I wasn't planning to." The woman looked embarrassed.

"Oh Wendy, please join us." Prue's smile was genuine as she pulled out a chair for the woman. It was easy to see how she had won over an entire village with her charming nature and genuine smile.

The party of five sat and feasted on the delicious treats in front of them, all talking about how excited they were for Prue's Christmas Day wedding.

"Austin came round last night." Katie almost choked on her scone as Maggie leaned over to whisper in her ear.

"I'm sorry, Maggie, I didn't mean to mess him around," Katie put down the remainder of her scone. She'd lost her appetite.

"Oh, you two will figure things out. I know he likes you and I saw your reaction just now." Maggie squeezed her hand. The gesture was full of concern.

"I do really like him, it's just bad timing for me."

"There's no such thing as good timing, lovely." Maggie smiled once more at her and then turned her attention back to the group, leaving Katie sat there feeling somewhat dumbstruck. Maggie made a good point. Did the perfect timing really exist? Now was not the time to be thinking about that. She cast Austin from her mind and made herself focus on the room - it was Prue's day.

After their delicious lunch at The Honey Pot, the group said goodbye to Wendy, and Carol announced that their next stop was the bookshop. Carol had a surprise waiting there for Prue. They walked across the road, Katie was wishing she had thought to pick up a jacket on their way out.

"Where are you girls off to?" They all turned to see Elliot stumbling out of the pub.

"None of your business! Austin, don't get your brother drunk. It's only just gone midday." Despite the chastisement, Katie could hear the amusement in Maggie's voice as she watched her three sons wave goodbye. Katie couldn't help but notice that Austin's eyes didn't leave her once, and she couldn't prise her eyes off of him. Could she really miss him already?

"Come on." Prue took her arm and led her towards the bookshop.

"Thank you. I think Elliot might have a sore head tomorrow." Katie joked, showing Prue that she was okay. She wasn't about to fall to pieces just because she had bumped into Austin in the street.

"There's the craft shop." Prue pointed to the shop, it was the street next to the bookshop. It looked beautiful, a similar size to the bookshop, and yet this shop was filled with pencils, pens, paints, canvases and every other crafty object that Katie could ever wish for.

"Oh Prue, I'm so excited! I can't thank you enough."

"Can't thank me? Katie, I'm not being entirely selfless in letting you have the shop, it means I get to have my best friend close again." Both girls stopped in their tracks and threw their arms around each other. Katie knew that piecing her life back together would be so much easier with Prue by her side.

"Come on, you two!" Carol called from the doorway of the bookshop. She was impatient to show Prue her surprise.

As they walked into the bookshop Katie felt an air of calm wash over her. It still felt like coming home. She wondered whether everyone felt this way in the bookshop. Judging by the smiles they did. The shop looked the same as when Katie had left it a couple of days ago; she wondered what the surprise was. Carol led them towards the big table in the middle, it was now adorned with cards filled with well-wishes from the residents of Ivy Hatch. In the middle sat a silk-covered box.

"Robert came to me with this a few days ago, not sure what to do with it. I knew immediately that you'd want it and so I thought now would be the perfect time to give it to you, especially since your mother couldn't be here." Carol's eyes had filled with tears and Katie stepped forward to take hold of Prue's hand. Whatever was in that box was going to make all of them cry.

"As you know, your mother and father's relationship was frowned upon and so they were planning on running away together, they were going to elope. Robert confessed that your mother had already started buying some wedding clothes and had given them to him for safekeeping. He came across this and as soon as I saw it, I knew you'd want it to wear on your big day." Carol leaned forward and slowly took the lid off of the box. The room was silent as everybody stared at its contents - nestled amongst the silk was a beautiful tiara, adorned with pearls. Katie turned to glance at Prue to see that there was a steady stream of tears running down her face.

"It's beautiful." Prue sobbed, stepping away from Katie and towards the tiara. She picked it up, her hands shaking. "Thank you Carol, I can't wait to wear it."

CHAPTER TWELVE

The group went straight from the bookshop back to the manor. Carol and Maggie were staying for another couple of hours before they headed home and left Katie and Prue to enjoy their evening. This was the part of the day that Katie had arranged and she was looking forward to seeing Prue's face when she discovered their first activity. There was a knock at the door and Katie got up to answer it. Standing on the other side of the door was a man. He towered above her with chestnut coloured hair and was wearing black jeans with a matching black shirt.

"Hello!" He greeted her as she opened the door.

"Hiya, I'm Katie, follow me, please." Katie led the man to the kitchen where the women were waiting. Carol let out of a whoop as they walked in.

"You got a stripper!" She cried, almost bouncing up and down in her seat. Katie had never seen a woman her age so excited over a man.

"I'm so sorry!" Katie turned to apologise to the man. She was mortified. "Carol, he's not a stripper! He's here to give us a cocktail making class, specifically some Christmas themed cocktails." Everyone in the room looked embarrassed at Carol's outburst, but they soon put it to one side as they watched the expert.

By the end of the session, they had learned to make spicy mulled gin, and Prue had learned how to pour a measure of gin that wasn't lethal to a lightweight. It had been lots of fun trialling all the different drinks and learning how to mix the cocktails. All too soon it was over and Carol and Maggie were leaving.

"I know you're organising this evening, but I've got us some matching pyjamas," Prue announced as soon as the door had shut behind Maggie and Carol. Katie rolled her eyes and followed Prue upstairs to change into their evening attire.

Katie let out a splutter of laughter as she saw the matching pyjamas that Prue had chosen. She had been expecting luxurious silk, instead lying on the bed were the most ugly pyjamas she had ever laid eyes upon. They were bright red, covered with little cartoon reindeers.

"What on earth are those?" Katie asked, imagining how well the red would clash with her hair.

"Come on, it'll be fun. It's just us, so at least nobody will see."

They changed into the awful pyjamas and Katie threw her hair up into a bun to lessen the clashing colours. Somehow, Prue pulled them off with her sleek dark bob bouncing as she walked back downstairs.

"We look awful," Prue commented, pouring them both a cocktail from the mix they had made earlier.

"They're comfortable, though." Katie shrugged her shoulders. She was warming to the awful pyjamas.

Katie had organised an evening of Christmas films and had even persuaded a restaurant in one of the adjoining villages to deliver their dinner. The night had been planned to remember the many nights they had spent in Brighton in a similar way. Katie had been expecting to feel nostalgic as they settled in front of the television and played their first film, instead she realised she was feeling excited for the future. She was on the brink of starting a new chapter of her life in a beautiful setting, a new job that would also allow her to indulge in her hobbies and best of all, she would be back with her best friend again. Perhaps she had been too hasty visiting Austin yesterday. Yes, her life was upside down, but she was also the happiest she had ever been, despite recently having her heart trampled. Everything happened for a reason, and perhaps she needed her life back in Brighton to be ruined to give her the push to move onto the next chapter of her life. Katie knew, without a doubt, that life in Ivy Hatch would make her much happier than life in Brighton ever could.

"You okay?" Prue asked, realising that Katie's attention was not on the film.

"I made a mistake ending things with Austin, didn't I?"

"Has it really taken you this long to realise?" Prue teased, throwing a handful of popcorn at Katie. They both laughed as it got caught up in her unruly hair.

"Well, I learned from the best. Remember when you broke up with Elliot because you thought the village would chase you out of town with pitchforks if you stayed together?"

"That was a minor blip!" Prue defended herself, whilst

helping Katie pick popcorn out of her hair - not a simple task when your hair resembled a bird's nest.

"Look where you are now! About to marry Elliot and an amazing landlady and business woman. I'm so proud of you, Prue." It was a soppy moment, but Katie wanted her friend to know how proud she was, for everything that she had achieved.

"Thank you, Katie. I'm so lucky to have you in my life. I know you put yourself down sometimes, but please don't. You're an amazingly strong woman and you're going to be running your own little empire soon. Hey, who knows, perhaps next year you and Austin will be having a Christmas Wedding?" Katie rolled her eyes at Prue's teasing. She doubted Austin would ever want to speak to her again.

CHAPTER THIRTEEN

Waking up the following morning was not a particularly pleasant experience. Despite Prue's new skill of pouring smaller measures of gin, they made up for it with more cocktails. Katie woke to a pounding head for the second day running. She would definitely be doing dry-January. A week with Prue and her liver was already crying for mercy. It had been fun though, after avoiding alcohol around Zac for so long it was nice to have fun again. To forget her inhibitions and embrace being herself.

Despite the pounding in her head, Katie knew that she had to perk herself up for the day ahead, after all it was Christmas Eve and her best friend was getting married tomorrow. With her hair still in last night's bun and her awful Christmas pyjamas on, Katie made her way downstairs. She could hear voices coming from the kitchen. As she stepped into the room, she wanted to turn around and run, Austin was sat at the table staring right at her.

"Morning!" Elliot announced from the stove where he was frying bacon.

"Please tell me that's for us!" Prue groaned, following Katie into the kitchen. She gave her a sly nudge to go and sit down at the table.

"I think we might be less hungover than you." Elliot

laughed, plating up the food.

"I think you might be." Prue sat down at the table, taking the seat opposite Austin so that Katie could sit next to her.

"I feel awful." Katie groaned, putting her head in her hands.

"Is that popcorn in your hair?" Austin spoke for the first time, and Katie wanted the ground to open up and swallow her. Of course he would notice the popcorn in her hair. She jumped as she felt his hand touch her head, he was picking it out for her. His touch was gentle and Katie couldn't help the smile that spread across her face. She was happy she still had her head in her hands so he couldn't see. She wondered why he wasn't shooting her angry looks and completely ignoring her. Did he realise their relationship had been doomed from the start? Perhaps he thought they still had a chance, and that was why he was being so nice to her? The most likely explanation was that Prue had explained to him how broken Katie was and he now understood her rash behaviour.

"Grub's up!" Elliot announced, putting the food on the table. Austin pulled away, and Katie couldn't help but feel a little disappointed at the loss of his touch. The feeling was quickly forgotten as she sunk her teeth into a bacon sandwich. It was just what she needed.

"What's the plan for today?" Katie asked, wondering if she and Prue had discussed it last night and she'd simply forgotten.

"Not much! We've got the decorators round this afternoon to transform the dining room for tomorrow. Other than that, we have a day to relax." Prue looked how Katie felt. She knew it must be bad since she had also come down in last night's pyjamas.

"Not much?" Elliot echoed Prue's words in astonishment. "We're doing Christmas Eve this evening! Then everyone is staying for the wedding tomorrow." Prue looked shocked at herself for forgetting this.

"I better make the most of a quiet morning." Katie made her excuses and went to run herself a bath. She wanted an excuse to get away from Austin for a moment. His eyes had barely left her the entire time she was sat there. Katie wanted nothing more than to throw herself into his embrace, but she knew she had to be certain it was what she wanted. It wouldn't be fair to mess Austin around again.

Katie didn't know how long she spent in the bath, all she knew was that her skin had shrivelled up like dried fruit by the time she got out. Thankfully, she had got the remaining popcorn out of her hair. With the rest of the afternoon stretching out in front of her, Katie decided to use the time to get ready for the evening celebrations. She dried her hair with Prue's hairdryer and then curled it. By the time she had finished it was soft and bouncy, nothing like the scruffy bird's nest that she usually let it style itself into. With her hair finished, she moved onto her make-up. She would never be one for a full face, and so she emulated the smoky-eye look she had done on her first date with Austin.

"Katie?" Prue's voice called through the closed door.

"Come in!" She called back, just finishing applying her mascara.

"Oh Katie, you look gorgeous." Prue was looking much more put together, her hair back in its signature sleek bob, her make-up flawless and wrapped in a silk dressing gown.

"Thank you, so do you."

"Now, you can say no, but will you promise me you'll look at it first?"

"Look at what?" Katie questioned. She was almost certain she knew where this conversation was leading, but she wasn't about to give in quite so easily.

"I got you a dress." The words tumbled out of Prue's mouth so quickly that Katie only just caught them. It was clear that Prue thought Katie would moan at being dressed up again. Little did she know, Katie had been stressing about what to wear for the last hour and was grateful that her friend had come to her rescue.

"Let's have a look." Katie smiled, standing up and tightening her dressing gown belt. The last thing she needed was to flash Austin before she had even decided what she was going to say to him.

Prue almost skipped along the hallway to her dressing room, Katie followed, unable to wipe the smile off of her face.

"Close your eyes!" Prue instructed as they walked into the room. Katie did as she was told and stood rooted to the spot with her eyes firmly shut.

"Okay, open!" Katie slowly opened her eyes and gasped at the dress that Prue was holding up. It was absolutely breathtaking.

"Do you like it?" Prue asked, for once her confident façade dropped and Katie saw the doubt on her face.

"Oh Prue, I love it!" Katie couldn't help herself, she threw her arms around her friend, hugging her tightly.

The dress was an off the shoulder style, fitted, the bottom half was like a pencil skirt and the entire piece was made from a deep wine coloured velvet. It was gorgeous.

"What are you wearing?" Katie asked, almost jumping up and down on the spot in anticipation of putting the dress on.

"You'll see! Go and put your dress on, I'll come get you in a minute." Without needing any further encouragement, Katie took the dress and half ran, half skipped back to her room.

The dress fitted perfectly, pulling her in at the waist and showing off her newly tamed hair. Katie barely recognised herself in the mirror. A beautiful and happy woman was staring back at her. Both Ivy Hatch and Prue were changing her but Katie wasn't upset, she was enjoying seeing the confident woman that she was finally blossoming into.

"Are you ready?" Prue asked, knocking on the door again. Katie went to open it and found herself speechless as she saw her friend stood in the doorway. Prue was dressed in a plum coloured, floor-length silk dress in the style of a slip.

"Prue, you look amazing." Katie finally came to her senses and complimented her friend. Perhaps she would allow Prue to dress her more often. Katie would always love her leggings and baggy jumper, but she saw that dressing up could be fun.

It was already dark outside, but the snow was softly falling and the stars twinkled in the sky. It was a magical Christmas Eve, and Katie was excited to spend it with her best friend and her best friend's new family.

"Shall we go downstairs?" Prue suggested, linking arms with Katie and leading her towards the stairs. As they descended, Katie noticed that Elliot and Austin were standing at the bottom, both wearing suits. Katie had to stop herself from rolling her eyes when she realised that Elliot's tie matched Prue's dress and Austin's matched her own. Prue was never much good at subtlety.

"Ladies!" Elliot greeted them, although his eyes didn't leave Prue's once. Katie couldn't help but notice that Austin's eyes were firmly fixed on her.

"You look beautiful." It came out as a whisper as Austin stepped forward to greet Katie.

"Thank you. You look rather handsome yourself." It felt natural to compliment him.

Before either of them could say anything more, the moment was ruined by a loud tapping at the front door. Ever the dutiful host, Prue went to let their guests in. They all made their way into the living room, which now resembled Santa's grotto. Elliot had been tasked with collecting everyone's presents and bringing them back to the manor, and so the tree was now surrounded with countless shiny packages, some wrapped up with bows, others simply wrapped in garish paper. Katie was sure that the flawlessly wrapped presents in brown paper with red silk bows were Prue's. She was also sure that the messily wrapped ones, with far too much Sellotape holding them together, were Austin's. Katie's own presents were wrapped in bright red paper and had a green bow wrapped around them. Her wrapping even rivalled Prue's. There were few things in life that Katie Wooster was passionate about, but Christmas was one of them.

"Shall we do presents first?" Prue asked as soon as they had all sat down.

"Give everyone a moment!" Elliot chuckled. "Why don't I get the drinks?"

Elliot took the orders and Prue went to help him, unable to sit still in a room filled with presents. One thing Katie and Prue had in common was their love for the festive season.

"Can I talk to you?" Austin leaned over and whispered in Katie's ear. A shiver ran up her spine at how close he was to her. Katie tried to find the words to say yes, but nothing came to her, instead she just nodded her head. Slowly, they stood up and left the room. Katie had been hoping that Maggie, Robert and Carol wouldn't notice but each set of eyes followed them as they left together.

"Let's slip outside, otherwise someone is always going to be listening to us." Katie grabbed one of Prue's coats from the rack by the door and ushered Austin outside.

As they stepped out into the night, the snow landed on them; it was cold but Austin's presence beside her meant that Katie barely noticed the wind whipping around her.

"Are you cold?" Austin asked, a look of concern crossed his face.

"I'm fine," Katie replied. She was eager to discover what he wanted to speak about.

"Katie, I know you said that you wanted to take it slow, but I'm not sure I can. Just being around you makes me light up, and I feel drawn to you. I'm a farmer, Katie, I'm not supposed to be sentimental but you've got me believing in soulmates and now I'm lost. You've turned my life upside down, you can't just walk away now." Austin's words came pouring out. His eyes held a vulnerability in them that Katie hadn't seen before. He was opening his soul up to her. Katie didn't need a moment to think or a second to rearrange her thoughts. In that moment she knew for sure she believed in soulmates and he was hers.

"I think I was wrong about asking you for space, I'm sorry. My life has been turned upside down and I've just found my feet again. Over the last couple of days I've realised what I want and how I see my future. I know for sure that I want you in it."

Austin's face lit up, as though Katie had just given him the best Christmas present, without even realising. He stepped closer to her, wrapping his arms around her. As the snow continued to fall around them they stood, oblivious, lost in each other's embrace, their lips pressed together.

"We should probably go back inside." Katie whispered, stepping away from Austin. She took hold of his hand and led him back into the house.

"That break up didn't last long!" Elliot teased as they walked back into the room holding hands.

"Some people are worth risking heartbreak for." Katie replied, squeezing Austin's hand in hers. Prue squealed from her seat beside Elliot and Maggie got up to embrace them both.

"He'll make you very happy," She whispered to Katie as she gave her a quick embrace.

"I know." Katie replied, she felt like the luckiest girl alive right now.

"Is it finally time for presents?" Prue huffed before slyly winking at Katie. She was doing her best to divert everyone's attention. It worked and soon everyone was exchanging gifts.

Katie sat back and watched everyone in the room, huge smiles on their faces, enjoying each other's company. It was a wonderful sight to behold and one that Katie never thought she'd be a part of.

"I wasn't sure whether I'd ever get to give you your present." Austin handed Katie a small, rather roughly wrapped box. Katie's hands shook slightly as she unwrapped the gift. Underneath the layers of Sellotape and awful paper was a beautiful leather jewellery box. With her hands still trembling, Katie lifted the lid and gasped. Nestled within the box were the beautiful emerald earrings that she'd fallen in love with whilst shopping with Austin.

"I thought you got these for Prue?"

"I could see how much you liked them and don't tell Prue but I think you'll suit them better."

Katie wasn't usually one for public displays of affection, but she couldn't help herself. She leant across the discarded paper to plant a kiss firmly on Austin's lips. All too soon they were interrupted by Prue.

"Oh Austin, these are gorgeous!" Katie glanced over to see Prue holding a similar box to hers, only nestled inside were a sapphire version of her own earrings.

"I thought they could be your something blue." He replied as the entire room fell silent. "What?" He asked, seeing everyone starting at him in shock.

"For a farmer, you've got excellent taste!" Robert joked, enjoying seeing his daughter looking so happy. The room erupted into laughter as Austin blushed.

"I'm very grateful for your good taste." Katie kept her voice low so that only Austin could hear her. He wrapped an arm around her shoulders and pulled her into his embrace. Katie knew for sure that this was a Christmas Eve she would never forget.

CHAPTER FOURTEEN

Waking up on Christmas Day was everything that Katie could have ever dreamed of, or asked Santa for. Austin was lying next to her and Katie felt the excitement fizz within her - not only was it Christmas Day but it was her best-friend's wedding. A knock on the door made her jump, she had lost herself in her thoughts.

"Hold on, let me just find my robe!" She called back, buying herself a few seconds. Austin was awake now, slowly recognising his surroundings. "You need to hide!" Katie whispered, flapping her hands around. They had snuck Austin into her room late last night. She didn't need anyone whispering about their relationship. Not yet, anyway.

"Where?" He replied, still half asleep and looking very dishevelled. Katie reminded herself to focus on the task at hand. Any second now Prue would burst through that door. This was not the start to the day that she had envisioned.

"Katie, give up. I know he's in there with you." Prue's voice came from the other side of the door and Katie sighed, half in relief and half in annoyance. Was nothing secret in this village? That was something she would have to adjust to.

"Come in," she called back. Katie knew for sure that her cheeks were the same colour as her hair as Prue walked into the room to see Austin still lying in the bed.

"Morning, sleepyheads!" Prue teased, glancing at the two of them.

"Did you just stop by to tease me?" Katie groaned. It was too early in the morning for this. She was realising why everyone around Prue Clemonte drunk litres of coffee each day.

"Nope. Hairdresser's here, meet me in my room in ten minutes. Austin, Elliot is expecting you at your mother's cottage."

Austin groaned from his spot under the duvet, clearly not enjoying his early wake-up call. For once he didn't have to be at the farm, he had Christmas off and then he would move into his own place. For now, though, he was in limbo, living between the manor and his mother's.

Prue left them to say their goodbyes. Katie reluctantly kissed Austin goodbye. She would be in for a few hours of pampering and she couldn't say a single bad word about it because it was Prue's big day. It was okay though, Katie was happy to do it for her friend, after all she was giving Katie the chance to start her life again.

With a glass of champagne in her hand, Katie sat back and allowed the experts to get her ready for the day. As they dried and styled her hair Katie's thoughts kept wandering back to Austin. The kiss that they had shared out in the snow last night had been so romantic, and everything about it had felt right. Until meeting Austin, Katie had never believed in soulmates, but now she was seeing how very wrong she had been in making such an assumption. It wasn't that soulmates didn't exist, she just hadn't met hers.

"You're ready!" The stylist announced, making Katie jump and almost slosh champagne down her beautiful robe. She could get used to being pampered, especially when she had Austin to keep her thoughts occupied. Katie thanked the stylist and then went to put on her dress so she was ready for when Prue needed help to get into hers.

The green velvet of her dress brushed against her skin and for the first time in her life Katie was excited to wear a dress. Last night's one had been gorgeous, but this dress was something else. It fitted her perfectly, just as it had done in the shop, only a few days ago. Katie thought to herself just how much had changed since then, her gorgeous new earrings twinkling back at her were a reminder of just how much her life had changed. The hairdresser had curled her hair and put it up in a delicate bun with a few curly tendrils framing her face, the perfect frame for her earrings.

Once dressed, Katie returned to Prue's room to find her ready to slip into her dress. Prue's hair had been perfectly curled into her signature vintage waves with her mother's tiara perched on top of her head. She looked beautiful with simple make-up, finished with bright red lips.

"Shall we get your dress on?" Katie asked, taking a deep breath to steady her emotions. Her best friend looked beautiful.

With Katie's help, Prue changed into her wedding dress. She looked a vision in with her 1940s hairstyle, vintage inspired dress, and her mother's tiara. The final touch were the earrings that Austin had bought her.

"You've got your dress, that's something new. Your mother's tiara, something old. The earrings that Austin got you are your something blue. What about your something borrowed?" Katie asked, ticking off each one on her fingers. She was not about to let Prue take any superstitious risks today.

"My bracelet is my something borrowed. It's the same one that auntie Carol wore on her wedding day." Prue teared up as she lifted her wrist to show Katie the delicate band around it.

"Don't you dare cry, Prue Clemonte. We've spent far too long in those chairs being made up for us both to ruin it!" Instead of crying, both women laughed.

"Oh Katie, I never thought I'd see this day."

"Elliot's a very lucky man. Come on, we better not leave him waiting for you." Katie took a hold of Prue's hand and together they made their way outside to where a driver was waiting with Prue's vintage Bentley. Robert stood waiting for them, holding Prue's bouquet. Katie had to take a deep breath before any stray tears rolled down her face - the bouquet was made up of blush peonies, Prue's grandmother's favourite.

"You look beautiful." Robert greeted his daughter with tears flowing down his face. He was no doubt thinking how proud her mother would be.

"Thank you, dad." Prue replied, giving him a hug. Katie felt honoured to be part of such a special moment. There was no time for too many tears. Prue and Robert climbed into the back of the car, whilst Katie took the seat next to the driver.

As they drove through the village, people were stood outside waving, and watching, as Prue made her way to the church. The car pulled up outside the church and Katie could barely believe how pretty it looked. Snow coated the ground, although it had finally stopped snowing, and an arch of peonies framed the entrance. Just noticeable in the background was the sign for *The Vintage Bookshop of Memories*.

Katie followed Prue down the aisle as she walked arm in arm with her father. Playing in the background was Unchained Melody by The Righteous Brothers. It had been Robbert and Prue's mother's favourite song. It took every ounce of Katie's self-control not to sob her way down the aisle, but Austin's eyes on her helped. Elliot's face lit up as his bride came to a stop by his side. They looked perfect together. Katie had an enormous smile on her face, she was so happy for her best friend. She was also happy for herself. Throughout the service she knew that Austin's eyes had barely left the back of her head.

All too soon, the service was over and the priest presented Mr and Mrs Clemonte to everyone. Elliot had proudly taken the Clemonte name, honouring Prue's heritage and to close the door on his father's archaic views on life. Arnold Harrington hadn't arrived at church, and Katie suspected that everyone was breathing a sigh of relief. The room had tensed considerably when the priest asked whether anyone knew of any reason they should not marry. Katie had half expected Arnold to come charging in with his pitchfork. Thankfully, he hadn't, and the ceremony had been beautiful. Robert had stood up and done a reading, telling Prue how proud her mother would be. There was not a dry eye in the room by the time he took his seat.

They all poured out of the church after Prue and Elliot, Austin made his way over to Katie and took hold of her hand.

"You look absolutely amazing." He leaned forward to kiss her.

"Thank you. You look very handsome." Katie couldn't help but notice that Austin's tie matched her dress, again.

The family gathered around for pictures, and Katie was shocked to find herself included. Not only was she Prue's best friend, but she was also Austin's partner. It was freezing outside, and the pictures seemed to go on forever, but Katie didn't mind; she had Austin next to her.

"I'm going to throw my bouquet!" Prue announced as she pulled Katie's hand to stand behind her. Only a few of the other girls from the village were standing with her. Katie could have died of embarrassment but as soon as Prue threw the flowers her reflexes kicked in and before she knew what she was doing, she had caught it.

"We're going to be sisters-in-law." Prue screamed, jumping up and down in pure glee. Katie couldn't help but glance over towards Austin to see what his reaction was. Some men would have looked terrified, but not Austin, he was stood there grinning. Maggie stood next to him and looked as though she was already planning her next mother-of-the-groom outfit.

"Can I have those back later?" Prue took Katie aside as they arrived back at the manor, ready to warm up and enjoy the feast that Wendy had been cooking up in the manor's kitchen.

"Of course." Katie looked down at the bouquet that she still had clutched in her hands.

"After dinner, Elliot and I are going to slip away. I'm going to visit my mother and grandmother and leave my bouquet with them."

"I'll leave it in the cupboard by the door so you can grab it whenever you want." Katie felt a lump in her throat, poor Prue having such a special day with neither her mother nor grandmother there for her.

"Prue, you're my best friend, you know that? Actually, you're not a friend, you're practically family."

"We've always been family Katie, ever since we first met in Brighton."

Both girls embraced as the wedding guests walked around them, making their way indoors, ready for the Christmas Day dinner that awaited them.

CHAPTER FIFTEEN

The handful of days between Christmas and New Year had passed in a blur of happiness and gin. Both the wedding and festive celebrations had continued - they had filled the manor with people. Katie had been enjoying every minute of each day, not thinking about the future and not worrying about the past. For a rare moment in her life, she was living in the present. It was unlikely to last, but she intended to make the most of it. It was New Year's Eve, and they were planning a final night of celebrations before normal life resumed. A marquee stood in the manor's garden, and the entire village had been invited to celebrate.

There was little left to do as Prue had hired party planners, knowing that planning a New Year's Eve party on top of a wedding would probably lead to a nervous breakdown. Elliot and Austin were visiting the new farm to ensure everything was ready for Monday's livestock delivery. Whilst Austin was away, Katie had thrown on some leggings, a baggy jumper, and had hidden herself away in a reading nook in the library. Enjoying the rare moment of peace and quiet.

"There you are!" Prue had found her.

"Sorry, just enjoying some alone time." Katie marked her page and closed the book.

"The old craft shop tenants have just dropped the keys off, which means we can have a nose around, if you want?" It was Katie's turn to squeal in excitement. She had definitely spent too much time around Prue.

"Yes, please!" She jumped up from her reading nook, and the two women made their way out to the cars.

Katie could barely contain her excitement as they walked up to the door, stopping outside. Prue turned and handed Katie the keys. "Go ahead, it's your shop." As much as Katie wanted to hug her friend, she wanted to look inside the shop and so she fumbled with the keys in her hand and unlocked the front door.

What she found inside was her idea of heaven. To the right was a wall filled with different coloured paints, paintbrushes and pencils; a rainbow of colours. The left wall was filled with drawers, each housing materials for different crafts. An oak counter stood towards the back of the shop, behind it were rolls of fabric and countless rolls of ribbon. The shop had everything a craft lover could ever dream of. Without saying a word, Katie made her way round to the other side of the counter where a beautifully upholstered stool stood waiting for her to perch on top of. There was enough room on the counter for her sketch pad, and if Katie rearranged the rolls of fabric and ribbon, she could even fit her easel behind her.

"What do you think?" Prue asked, her eyes glistening as she watched her friend take in her surroundings.

"Prue, I don't think I'll ever be able to thank you enough."

"Katie, I don't want your thanks. We've supported each

other for years now, through university, the first years in our jobs, and you were the only person I could turn to when the people of Ivy Hatch turned on me. We're family, remember? We'll always look out for each other." This time Katie did throw her arms around her best friend.

"Come on, we have a party to get ready for!" Katie groaned, although she was secretly looking forward to being Prue's doll for the afternoon. Prue, being Prue, had set a theme for the party - the roaring 20s. She had ordered them flapper dresses from a boutique a couple of villages away and she was planning on giving Katie a full 1920s make over.

By the time the first guests arrived Prue had completely transformed them both. Katie's hair was pinned and coiffed within an inch of its life so it now resembled a faux bob. Meanwhile, Prue had curled her own hair into 1920s style waves. They were both wearing feathered headbands. There were no half measures with Prue Clemonte around. Their dresses were traditional flapper dresses, Katie's was green, whilst Prue's was plum coloured. They matched and yet the subtle differences in their appearance effortlessly reflected their differences in personalities.

The marquee was filled with people, all laughing, drinking and enjoying their night. It was so lovely to see Prue being welcomed by everyone. Katie realised that she was also being welcomed into the village, after all it was now her new home. She still needed to find somewhere to live but at least she had a job. She also had a boyfriend. That hadn't been part of the plan.

"Why do I get the feeling you're starting to enjoy playing dress-up with Prue?" Austin handed her a glass of champagne and wrapped his free arm around her waist.

"I am, but I'm also looking forward to throwing on a baggy jumper and some leggings tomorrow morning."

"Do you want to come over to the farm tomorrow for a tour?"

"I'd love to, but it'll have to be in the afternoon. I'm looking at a cottage in the next village tomorrow morning." Katie had wanted to stay in the village but she was already taking advantage of Prue and she knew that Prue wouldn't accept any rent from her.

"You could… I mean…" It wasn't often that Austin Harrington was shy, or awkward, but right now he was both.

"What?" Katie asked, wondering what had got him into such a flap.

"Why don't you move into the farm with me?" That was one of the last things Katie had been expecting him to say. Could she really move in with him so early in a relationship? She thought for a moment. Why not? She already had a strong feeling that he was her soulmate. Why waste time when they could be together?

"I'd love to!" Katie threw her arms around Austin's neck and kissed him.

The countdown to midnight played out in the background.

"5… 4… 3… 2… 1!" Someone shouted towards the back of the marquee.

"Happy New Year!" Austin pulled away from her lips, just enough to murmur the celebration.

"Happy New Year!" Katie replied before leaning back in to kiss Austin.

The End.

THANK YOU FOR READING

I hope you enjoyed the story and I'm sorry that you now have to return to reality.

I would appreciate it if you would take the time to leave a review on Amazon and/or Goodreads.

Merry Christmas!

Keep reading for the first chapter of The Vintage Bookshop of Memories...

THE VINTAGE BOOKSHOP OF MEMORIES

By Elizabeth Holland

CHAPTER ONE

Prue smoothed the creases out of her charcoal pencil skirt as she stood up from the church pew. She looked around the small room to see the handful of people that had gathered, all wiping tears from their eyes. It was a bright but cold Wednesday in April and the cemetery was the last place Prue wanted to be. As she glanced around at the mourners Prue wondered how many of them had really known her grandmother. The entire village knew the name Elizabeth Clemonte and yet so few had known the real woman behind the name.

'Prudence, how lovely to see you.' Prue was pulled from her thoughts by the voice of an elderly man. She looked up to see the vicar smiling down at her, he had known Prue her entire life and had even been the one to baptise her. Everyone knew everyone in the little village that she had once called home, they especially knew you if you lived in the big house on the hill. Otherwise known as 'Clemonte Manor'. The village, Ivy Hatch, was nestled amongst the rolling hills of Somerset and was mostly unknown. Each summer a handful of tourists would stumble upon the sleepy village but other than that the only visitors were from local towns or villages.

Prue politely returned the vicar's smile and engaged in

some small talk, all the while she just wanted to get out of the stuffy church. Although Prue had been too young to remember her own mother's funeral she had grown up to be somewhat afraid of God's house. The little church was a reminder that she had grown up without a mother by her side. It was only the church that made her feel that way though, the graveyard surrounding it only evoked feeling of peace and contentment. Prue had many fond memories of visiting the graveyard with her grandmother over the years. Each week they would visit the Clemonte mausoleum, that hour spent in the graveyard was the closest Prue ever felt to her grandmother.

Once outside in the cemetery Prue felt her shoulders relax. The few attendees of the funeral service were milling around outside, unsure what to do next. Following her grandmother's wishes Prue had not arranged a wake, both her and her grandmother knew that the majority of the village would come along just to satisfy their curiosity and to see the inside of the Clemonte manor. Prue cast her gaze up to the hill above the village to where her home lay. At least it was once her home, before she went to university, and now it would become her home again.

Only a week ago, Prue had received a call from her grandmother's doctor telling her to come quickly. She had packed up all of belongings and left her house share in Brighton to return to the little village she had once called her home. Prue always knew this day would come, she had just hoped it would be a long way in the future. Despite her grandmother's lack of maternal instinct, she had been the only family member Prue had left. So now at the age of twenty-four Prue was Lady of the Manor with an entire village watching her to see what her next move would be. She knew the residents of Ivy Hatch saw her as an entitled snob, however in reality she was far from it. That's why Prue had loved living in Brighton, nobody had batted an eyelid at how different she was. Her love for 1940s fashion always made her stand out from the crowd. Today, her glossy black hair was in pin curls, one side swept back to show off her petite features. She had dressed for her grandmother's funeral in her favourite pencil skirt and matching jacket with a crisp white shirt underneath. Perhaps she had gone a step too far with her lace gloves, black parasol and a black fascinator, complete with a birdcage veil. It was a little over the top but she knew her grandmother would have appreciated her dressing properly for the occasion. Despite their differences Prue's fashion sense was something that she had inherited from her grandmother who had insisted on dressing up for every occasion.

Prue was acutely aware of the villagers watching her from afar, all whispering about how indifferent she thought she was. If only they could have seen what her life had been like in Brighton, living in a house share with eight other people and spending her days working at the local auction house as a valuer. She had worked hard to forge a career for herself but here she was, back at the manor. Her grandmother's dying wish had been for her to move home, on her deathbed she had reminded Prue the importance of keeping their family name alive. There was also the responsibility of owning the majority of the village.

Relief washed over Prue as she spotted the black hearse pull up, ready to take her home. As her heels clicked on the path below her she held her head up high, thanked the vicar and made her way over to the car. She knew that every pair of eyes were on her, ready for her to mess up in some way. You see the villagers had never liked the Clemontes, they were a reminder of a class system that everyone but Prue's grandmother wanted to forget. However, there were still the odd few who worshipped the system and believed that the Clemontes should be treated differently, Prue didn't much like those people. Even as a child Prue had wondered why everyone couldn't be treated as equals. It was a delicate line to tread and Prue would need to strike a balance between respecting the old fashioned ways whilst also bringing the village into the present.

For now though, all Prue wanted to do was go home and cry, and so she stepped into the hearse ready to go back to the manor. It may have been too big for just her but at least it somewhat felt like home, after all it was all she had ever known. Prue looked out of the window as they passed the back of the cemetery, even from the road she could see the Clemonte family mausoleum. She lifted her hand and gave a small wave towards her mother's resting place. Oh, she would give almost anything to still have her mother by her side, telling her what to do next.

The hearse drew up to the manor and Prue thanked the driver before getting out and walking up the few steps to the front door. With an ominous creak, Prue pushed open the heavy door and walked into the sparse hallway. Despite her grandmother's lack of maternal instinct she had still been family. She may not have hugged Prue but she always made sure there were staff available to give Prue everything she needed. A single tear fell from Prue's eye as she glanced up at a family portrait, the only one of her grandmother, her mother and her. Prue was only a baby in this picture but she wanted to believe that she still remembered that day. A day when she was surrounded by family.

As another tear fell from her eye, Prue locked the door behind her and headed up to her bedroom, she had a long day ahead of her tomorrow. Prue had been summoned by her grandmother's solicitor. Over the phone he had told Prue that she was the sole heir to the Clemonte estate, however he wanted to see her face-to-face to discuss some of the finer details. With this in mind Prue changed out of her funeral attire and into her emerald green silk pyjamas and climbed into her bed. The room was styled to suit Prue's eclectic taste, it was as if you had stepped back in time into the art deco period. It was Prue's solace in a house that seemed so cold and distant. As Prue's head hit the pillow more tears fell from her eyes, her life had been completely turned upside down and here she was, back in a village where everyone despised her for no fault of her own. Life wasn't going to be easy over the next few months.

Printed in Great Britain
by Amazon